The Tent

Miral al-Tahawy

THE TENT

A Novel

Translated by
Anthony Calderbank

The American University in Cairo Press

Translator's Introduction

Bedouin have been coming into Egypt's Eastern Desert for as long as anyone can remember. Long before the Arab armies that brought Islam to Egypt with Amr Ibn al-Aas, tribes had migrated from the deserts of the Arabian Peninsula and Greater Sham (Syria, Jordan, and Palestine) overland through Sinai, or across the Red Sea, to the mainland of Africa. Thus the Bedouin of Egypt's Eastern Desert have been in contact with the peasants of the Nile Delta for many centuries.

In the nineteenth century, both French and British observers commented on the unique position of the Bedouin in Egyptian society. Fiercely independent and resentful not only of foreign control but of any suggestion of central authority, the Bedouin were always treated with care, being granted a degree of autonomy which was not extended to the rest of the population. Bedouin, for example, were exempted from military service, compulsory for other Egyptian males, although the tribal chieftains were expected to muster men when instructed to do so by the Palace. During the last century Muhammad Ali granted feudal lands to some of the more powerful tribes, and areas of the Eastern Delta, together with the peasants who lived on and farmed the land, passed into the hands of Bedouin lords. Fatima, the main character and narrator of this story, is the daughter of one such Bedouin lord.

Such measures, together with their radically differing ways of life, brought about considerable resentment between these nomads of the desert and the peasants whose ancestors had farmed the Delta for thousands of years. Peasants tilled the land, cultivated fruit and vegetables, and reared buffalo and cows, while the Bedouin roamed the desert with their herds of sheep and goats, rarely cultivating any crops, and living proudly on their traditional austere diet of *nawashef* (dry things) such as cheese, dates, and bread. The sedentary farmers were suspicious of the Bedouin and their mysterious relationship with the desert, a landscape they as agriculturalists were unable to master; they were also bitter over the privileges that had been granted to the Bedouin over themselves. And since the Bedouin rarely used money, they were suspicious of, and intimidated by, the commerce of their Egyptian neighbors.

The Bedouin kept their women covered up and out of sight, while the peasant women worked and showed their hair and wore galabiyas with low necks that revealed their cleavages as they worked. Grandmother Hakima's views on peasants are in no need of elaboration. Nor are her opinions on the female sex in general. Girls are a great burden with enormous potential for shame, disappointment, and dishonor. Musallam too is obsessed with his daughter's honor. He conceals her, and his desire to bury her evokes the pre-Islamic practice of burying unwanted baby girls in the sand. (The importance the Bedouin place on honor is attested by the story of a young man who was burned alive in Sharqiyya in the 1950s by the family of a girl who was suspected of having a romantic liaison with him.) The women's quarters are a reflection of these beliefs and it is there, where the lives of the servants and slaves and their Bedouin mistresses are lived out, that Fatima's story takes place.

Behind the closed gate, secluded from men and the outside world, Fatima lives with her mother and three sisters: Safiya, the eldest, and Fouz and Rihana. Sardoub, Sasa, and Sasa's mother are slaves, proba-bly of Sudanese or Nubian origin. Despite their bondage they live on much closer terms with their mistresses than the servants, who have no names, and play little part in the tale. Ironically, while Sasa can nip down to market every week, it is unlikely that any of the sisters will pass through the main gate unless they are going to a wedding, lest their very presence in the street bring down shame upon their good name and that of their father. Mouha is a gypsy and can come and go as she pleases. Sigeema, Musallam, and Zahwa, the other characters who share Fatima's life, come from the Bedouin folk stories that she hears from Sardoub, and which she eventually comes to inhabit herself. Zahwa is also the genie that lives at the bottom of the well.

Many other traditional elements are woven into Fatima's madness. The stories of Na'sh and his seven daughters (the constellation of Orion), and the Virgin Mary (Venus, the morning star), who, wrongly accused by her people, must take up her newborn child and flee and seek shelter in Egypt, hang eternally in the night sky, and Fatima misses them sorely when she moves in with Anne. Fatima's fear for Zahwa's life blends the dreaded reputation of the horned viper, whose bite requires instant amputation of the smitten limb, with the belief that Zahwa, Fatima's sister from among the genies, will suffer the same fate as herself. As Fatima's sanity deteriorates, the lines that separate the mythical from the real become ever more blurred.

I would like to add a final linguistic note. The English language lacks the grammatical and morphological devices to express the feminineness that the Arabic language enjoins upon this text. There is no 'women's n' *(nun al-niswa)* in English, no feminine plural endings, no feminine nouns and adjectives, and it is hard to recreate the scent of woman that permeates the Arabic original of *The Tent*.

To my body . . .
a tent peg crucified in the wilderness

Chapter One

Little stone, I put you there to guard their door,
And where are they now,
The dear ones who lived here once before?

Every time I closed my eyes I found them. Every
time I surrendered my thick, long hair to Sardoub's
tender hand they moved before me in silence. It
was as if I had leapt over the high wall, and flown
away, moving in and out between the farm
buildings until I reached the open land beyond the
houses and the wide mud walls. There were the
green pastures, and the mountain and the low hills. I
watched Mouha tending her goats, and I rode the
donkey, and I ran and ran across the desert until I
saw the seven palm trees. Here was the oasis of
Musallam and Zahwa and Sigeema and the little
slave.

I looked out from under the mosquito net. The
ceiling seemed a long way off. I looked at Safiya
dozing quietly. Her face shone like the moon, and
her leg sticking out from underneath the cover was
milk-white and plump. Her cheeks were still red

and fresh. I wanted to embrace her. She looked exactly like my mother, except that she was larger and more radiant, or perhaps my mother had been like her before her spark went out. I contemplated her face and then moved away. I liked the idea of watching sleeping faces, for I always found it so difficult to sleep myself. I lifted up the other mosquito net and breathed in their smell: Fouz and Rihana lay in one another's arms, sharing their secrets. I was furious. Even in their sleep they had secret conversations which I could not join in. I put the net back in its place and sat down on the floor between the beds.

I thought of running away again. There were three huge, open summer windows which reached almost to the ceiling like huge doors, but there were intertwining iron bars on them. Nothing could come in except the mosquitoes, which buzzed voraciously. Nothing could get out except anxious breath.

I crept through the half-open door. Maybe I would be able to pull back the bolt of the main gate. The thought disturbed me. It was far too heavy for me to even imagine opening it. I crept back, and on the way I came across Sardoub lying under her cover on the rug in the front hall. Sasa was curled up in her arms, and their bodies were hidden under the great table. Above it the burner gave out a faint light. I pulled Sasa away and moved her slightly to one side. Then I edged my own body into Sardoub's embrace. I felt for her arm and rested my head upon it. Her breathing was warm and undisturbed, and her hand stroked my hair. Her eyes were still closed, but she patted me gently on the back and at last sleep came.

In the morning, like all other mornings, I found myself back in my own bed, with Safiya violently undoing my plaits. Then, despite my screams of protest, she dragged me toward the water. She was shouting at me: "Sleeping like a dog anywhere you like, playing with Sasa and sleeping with Sardoub, you little pup!"

She thrust my head into the bowl, poured water over my hair, and rubbed it into the roots. It hadn't been cut once in all my five years, and it always hurt me so much when she washed it. She wrapped it in a towel and pushed me back to the bed, where she braided my plaits. Sometimes she cut my nails and pressed ground kohl into my reddened eyes.

It would be a morning like all previous mornings, full of tension and anxiety. Either my mother wouldn't open the door of her room, or, if she did open it, she would watch us with apprehensive eyes. Her pale, emaciated figure, the thin veins on her eyelids, and her nose swollen from floods of tears, choked my heart with sadness.

I sat on Sardoub's sheepskin rug between the kitchen and the storerooms. Fouz and Rihana were having a whispered conversation on their bed. They laughed and then went back to sorting through the cuttings of old clothes and scraps of material and darning needles. My mother's door was closed. Safiya opened it slowly and took in a brass jug and a small bowl. Sasa followed her with a covered tray.

Safiya set down the bowl of water and started to rub my mother's feet. I crept into the room and saw the exhaustion in her helpless eyes. I moved closer and the sight of her filled me with pity. She cupped my face in her hands and burst into tears. I fled from the room, from the stench of her tears.

I lay my head in Sardoub's lap and she began to undo my plaits. In the stillness Musallam came down across the nearby plain. He was tall and thin and life's hardships had carved deep furrows on his taut, noble cheeks. His tough, lean hands could sharpen jagged rocks.

Sigeema sat down on the ground and set up her milk churn between two poles. Her face glowed with color. The gurgling of the milk as it churned echoed through the silence. Zahwa leaned against the nearby palm tree, following the last rays of the sun as they anointed her white cheek with bright glowing flame. I moved toward her: "Why are you sad, ya-Zahwa?"

She didn't hear me. She gazed into the distance, and then with her finger drew crucified figures writhing in the sand. I watched on in admiration and handed her sharp stones and date stumps while she made her pictures. She drew and did not speak to me. She stopped when she grew bored and stretched her body. Night was falling. She walked away and the soles of her feet left no mark on the ground. The hem of her dress brushed over the sand and no trace of her remained.

My hair lay in Sardoub's lap as she combed out the knots. My head went round and round, looking for a way to escape.

I heard the creak of the main gate and jumped to my feet. I ran to the verandah and stood at the top of the steps. I saw them running toward the gate. The servant rushed forward to pull back the wooden bar.

"Has he come back?"

It wasn't the time of the herd, the sun was still on the horizon! The gate was only opened twice a day. Once in the morning before sunrise and then again after sunset. I would sit at the top of the steps and watch the horses wander out of the yard, followed by the sheep and goats. Only Khayra would remain on the farm. She was still young: "A stubborn filly," as Sardoub used to say when she fed her. She wouldn't stop whinnying until the sugar lump was melting in her mouth. I wanted her to become pure white, and her black mane and even blacker tail upset me. I wondered what would happen if I cut them off.

"He'll break your neck."

Had he come to see something? He never came back except to leave again, and when he left he stayed away for a long time. Had he really come back? Would his black mare, which he wanted to remain without a name, be neighing? The main gate was opened and the mare trotted up the path. He was back. I thought, Should I run toward him?

"Greetings! How's father's little gazelle?" The *igaal* around his head, the headcloth which hung down either side of his face, his long nose, his beard; nothing had changed. I looked at him.

"Fatima, Fatima, my little darling, has someone annoyed you?" This time he was in an excellent mood. He kissed me many times, then picked me up and carried me inside. They were waiting for him. Safiya stepped forward and kissed his hand. Fouz came after her, then Rihana, bowing their heads submissively.

"Why don't you kiss them?"

"Ya-Fatima, they've grown up. When they were little I used to carry them on my shoulder, like you."

"I don't want to grow up, ya-Mama Sardoub, I don't want to grow old."

She stroked my hair and told me a story: "The sun goes round in the sky, and becomes a circle. The sun is a girl and like all other girls she has seven faces and then there is a long night when she buries her last face, the pock-marked face of an old woman lamenting and wailing. Then she runs away behind the Mountains of Oblivion, the mountains of iron and fire. Between us and them are two dams and a well of molten iron which the sun falls into."

"Who? Who, ya-Mama Sardoub?"

"The Pharaohs, and the slaves of the cannibals of Namnam and Gog."

I heard the gate creak again. Sasa went outside and walked over to the guest house and the camel shed. I went back inside to look for him, but I couldn't find him. Only the sound of sobbing came from her room. His return always made her cry. "Why doesn't she love him like I do? Why doesn't she ever leave that dark room?"

When Fouz called me "stupid" for asking such a question, Safiya slapped her hard in the face. Fouz didn't look Safiya in the eye for a long time after that. I got the same answer later on from Grandmother Hakima.

It was Grandmother Hakima who was coming in now. She too had the main gate opened for her. Everyone was waiting. She was thin, lighter than him. Gold-capped teeth shone in her mouth and it looked like the mouth of a demon. Her dark-blue garment never changed. Only the cloak, which she alone among the women wore, was ever different. Was she really a woman? She was the mother of us all. Our great demon mother who wrapped herself in men's scarves. She prodded her huge old mare. Behind her the slave led a donkey with two saddlebags. Then came two lads, plowing the sand with their flat, slab-like feet. Everyone stood there as she approached the gate. She prodded the horse and moved toward us. The donkey swung its ears, and the rest of her entourage remained outside the gate. No doubt they would stay across the way where the tents of goat hair were set up.

Safiya was the first to rush up and kiss her hand. The rest of the household followed suit and she haughtily extended her black, wizened hand to each of them. Her eyes probed everything around her. She shoved her feet into her sandals, gathered up her cloak, and went into the house. When she took off her cloak her garment shone with gold. A belt, or *hiyasa* as she called it, was tied round her waist, full of gold disks and heavy coins. Her curved back bent slightly forward. She pulled up her wide sleeves to reveal rows of bangles and bracelets about the blackened veins on her wrists. Even without taking her shoes off, the gold anklets looked mean and insignificant amid the scrawny tendons and the bulging ankle bones.

I watched her from a distance. I didn't like her. With that stick which she used to prod her mare, she would poke about in everything: in my sisters' cupboards, the chests in the storeroom, the jars of butter and cheese, not to mention the crates of provisions and the bird pens. She would count the ducks which had hatched and the baby pigeons whose fluff had sprouted, and she would open all the grainstores to check that the worms hadn't gotten at them, or that the women hadn't had their hands in them. Safiya scrambled along nervously in front of her, taking orders.

"The rooms need cleaning!" "The beans are for the animals." "Don't kill any of the pigeons. There aren't enough for your father's shooting. If he protests, give him one of the little zaghlouls."

She went back and took her place at the center of the gathering on a thick, filled cushion. She crossed her legs and started to roll a cigarette.

When he came she continued rubbing the tobacco, and with a sly glint in her small narrow eyes she asked him about his journey and his grazing lands. He sat in front of her meekly. It was as if I had never seen his chest swollen with pride, or the people move aside in awe as he walked past. He opened the box.

"What have you brought?"

She stuck her hand in among the square bars of scentless soap and went through the pieces of material. His coffee bubbled on the heat, and thin young Sasa poured some into Grandmother Hakima's cup and then into his. Then the old woman screamed in her hoarse voice:

"You girls, you miserable creatures, come here!"

Safiya stepped forward.

She carried on in the same disapproving tone that was vicious for no reason: "My God, you're a wretched bunch! God has sorely tried your father and he's been patient."

She looked at him, but he didn't seem to care. She threw into each girl's lap a piece of soap, some cloth, and for some a bottle of shining green olive oil with herbs in it. She piled up my mother's share on one side and then glared at Safiya and said: "This is for the deranged woman. By God, it's a sin to waste the stuff on her! She's given birth to nothing but bad luck."

Fouz and Rihana ran to their room. They paid no attention to anything she said. They called her "Grandmother Stupid." All they cared about was the pattern on the cloth, or its blackness or its gleaming milk-white tint. Tomorrow they would start to cut up and embroider. The chest in their room was full of dresses and tablecloths.

Safiya put her portion away without doing any work on it. She took my share, and my mother's, and put them in the big cupboard. She seemed sadder and more resigned. That night she went to her bed and ranted in her sleep: "May God take you! You don't know night from day. You're the one who's deranged. Wicked old crow! Four girls and three boys. What can she do? What can she do against the will of God and your poisonous eyes. By God, it's you who's put the eye on them! You and no one else, you old witch."

I asked her: "Were there three?"

She didn't answer.

"Where have they gone?"

She turned her back to me and started to sob. "They've gone away, gone away."

"Will they come back like he does?"

"They've gone to their Lord."

"Won't they ever come back? . . . Why doesn't Grandmother Hakima go to her Lord and never come back?"

"She'll break your neck."

Even if she couldn't hear me she was going to break my neck one day. Her vicious gold teeth followed me in my dreams and filled me with terror. I would run and run and then fall into a bottomless well and I would feel my body plunging deeper and deeper.

Musallam let his bucket down the well, while I hung onto the rope, dangling in the air. He emptied the bucket in front of his camel's trough. Sometimes people passed through. He would hide Zahwa from them, as the Pharaohs hid their treasure in mountain caves and carved magic idols around them.

One day a party approached, their horses neighing restlessly under the weight of the booty. From beneath the shade of his palm trees they filled the air with the smell of grilled meat, churned milk, and coffee. Soon they would fill their water skins from the well and depart. They unwrapped their scarves from their faces and chuckled amid their stories. Musallam neither loved them nor hated them. They recounted their glorious deeds over the simple feast, and talked about the desert and the Bedouins and the tribal wars. They asked Musallam about the rain and the gazelles, and told jokes about the soldiers in the valley and cursed their wicked acts. One of them noticed the folds of skin hanging on Musallam's face and asked him: "How long have you been out here, old man, Sheikh of the Arabs, on the caravan routes, far from the settlements?"

Musallam shook his head and motioned over his shoulder with the palm of his hand, and they all understood that it was too long to be reckoned. He was a quiet man and spoke very little. He never told them anything.

"Which tribe are you from?"

He stroked his beard and said nothing, so they played line games on the sand and searched under the seven palm trees for date stones to use as counters. He kept the fire burning and made coffee after coffee.

"From the west or the east?"

Every time they came through they asked him, but he never answered. When he was in a good mood he would sing, and the stars would glitter to his songs. The visitors scrutinized the ground and laughed mischievously.

"Have you got a girl here?"

To this question only he would reply: "I have my wife. She's as light-footed as a gazelle."

They looked more closely at the tracks. "She's a pretty, buxom young thing!"

"She still has some life left in her, and youth appears now and again like a mirage."

They laughed as Zahwa peered through a gap in the side of the tent. It had grown; every year Sigeema would spin and weave and add a new compartment. Zahwa watched the travelers with bewilderment in her eyes as they filled their skins from the well and moved off. Cautiously Musallam bade them farewell just as he had received them. Then he threw the dregs of the coffee onto the embers. They left him an old female falcon which they said had fallen into their baggage. They hammered a peg into the ground for her in front of the tent and she went round in circles at the end of the tether. When Zahwa came out she saw that her eyelids had been stitched closed and her wings trussed up her back. She looked at the bird and was silent.

"Let's untie her," I said.

She didn't answer and I tried to move closer. Sigeema said: "The bird is wounded."

I didn't think she was wounded, though. She was just an old wild hen, blind and in irons. I reached forward. I just wanted to pull out the stitches from her eyelids and look at her eyes, but Zahwa pulled back my hand. "If she sees the sky she'll go mad. Leave her," she said. And she watched Musallam as he went about the camp.

When night fell there was only Sardoub's lap to go to. I lay down my head and she told me a story: "Seven daughters Na'sh had, seven girls. The desert was bleak and desolate and the ground was soft and treacherous. How would they hide their tracks? And the Virgin took her newborn child and fled across the sky after they had pelted her with stones."

Outside the net, which hung over the four posts and dangled down on every side, the night hummed with mosquitoes. I sat down on the middle windowsill. It was wide enough for me if I pushed the stand for the clay water jugs to one side and curled up next to it. I could see the domes where the grain was stored standing in a row by the high wall. Not even the heavy rains could damage that wall. All they did was make the black mud run down over the whitewash so that it looked like the furrows on an old mulberry tree. The domes were made of mud and each one had a small opening just above the ground. The yard was completely empty except for the sycamore tree near the bird pens. On the other side were the stables and feeding troughs for the cows and buffalo. The stables ran all along the wall as far as a small lean-to, where the goats and sheep huddled. Had any of them left its shelter, it would soon have got entangled in the brambles and long grass, which grew everywhere, and died without anyone paying any attention, let alone daring to plunge into the thorns and free it. In any case they were surrounded on all sides by the wall, which, where they were, was unpainted and black.

At the far end of the yard was the main gate, which was wide enough for a whole train of camels. No one person, however great his strength, could budge it on his own. One servant would pull the latch while another held onto him from behind and a third heaved on the rope. The small door at its center, however, which looked like a window in a wall, had a bolt high up. It was light enough for Sasa to pull open whenever she came and went. The surrounding wall, Safiya told me, had been without a single plant until quite recently, when my father brought those plants that had grown so quickly. He had called them busianus. Sardoub called them sasaban.

They said he was the first one to bring them, but I saw them afterwards in Anne's house. They used to call her the Madame, and her house was my story, which I would tell to everyone I ever met. Safiya would listen uninterestedly, but Sardoub laughed, and Fouz and Rihana were so astonished that you'd think I was reciting magic spells. Some time later they planted mastic and lemon trees down at the far end of the yard, but they were too far away, and were separated from our end of the courtyard by the thorns and wild grass that I was afraid of. I made do with climbing the sasaban trees. Sardoub said: "You little ape."

Safiya said: "You'll break your neck."

I climbed the trees whenever my father was away or had gone out to hunt. Through the branches I could see the front of the house, the buildings across the road, the camels resting, and the guest house with its mud walls which were blackened by smoke like the bottom of a kettle that sits in the fire. It was surrounded by a line of wooden columns that descended from the roof and met the railing not far off the ground. The guest house was beautiful; if it hadn't been for the smoke that had eaten away at the wood, it would have looked like a huge ship. Father's goat-hair tent was pitched next to it whenever he was home, and around the tent were spread red Persian carpets. Beyond the sasaban trees was an expanse of rich black earth, and in the distance plots of green covered the land. The peasants were there. Sometimes I heard them singing and saw them strolling gracefully in their brightly colored clothes.

The sun glanced the tops of the hills along the horizon and the sand dunes reflected its dazzling rays. Finally I had found something to do. I came down from the treetop into Sardoub's folded lap, where I lay my head for a while and dozed off. I felt I was falling deeper and deeper into a bottomless well.

Through my half-sleep I heard the voices of Mouha and Sasa. I watched them sitting together, their backs propped against one of the mud domes where the grain was stored. I walked over, but they went on talking to one another. Mouha had a pile of dark-colored wool in her lap which she was twisting into long braids. Sasa was fiddling with some scraps of material which she had collected from the leftovers of the dressmaking. "Mouha, what are you doing?"

She didn't answer, but her narrow, shining eyes smiled slyly in her red face. She bit her lower lip and her two large front teeth left marks in the skin, which she licked with her tongue. I sat down next to her. Sasa got out her comb and said: "I won't give it to you until I see."

Mouha didn't reply. She licked her lips and smiled. Sasa undid her plaits, plunged them into the bucket, then started to comb them. I sat down on the floor, resting my face in the palms of my hands, wondering what they were doing. Mouha came and dipped her hands in the water and started to plait, one, two, three, five braids. She tugged cruelly at the short frizzy hair as she made the plaits. Then she got out her dark woolen braids and wove them into Sasa's hair. Mouha smiled slyly and licked her rosy red lips. When she had finished, there was one long dark plait hanging down Sasa's back. Mouha moved on to the other side while Sasa held the plait in her hand and laughed with joy. When both plaits were finished Sasa ran over to show them to Sardoub, and then ran back. Mouha gathered up her colorful scraps of cloth, wound them round her finger and thrust them into the small pouch which hung at the

back of her neck. She laughed the same laugh and
Sasa embraced her and they splashed water on one
another and shrieked loudly.

"Mouha . . . where are you going? Play with me."

She looked at me indifferently, then she left me.
As she went out, I ran toward the tree and climbed
right up to the top. I could see her get scraps of
material out of her bag and hand them out to the
little girls who were gathered around her. They
unfolded the scraps and hid them away. Mouha
mounted her donkey, sidesaddle she rode, and
shoved the scraps into the saddlebag. She whistled,
and the little girls drove the goats and sang the songs
which were so familiar to the desert, and which the
flocks knew so well. Sasa had learned them from
her friendship with Mouha, this red Gypsy girl who
roamed the wilderness. Mouha became a speck in
the distance as I jumped from tree to tree. Her
dress was tied up and her trousers were spattered
with goat dung and the smell of churned milk. She
wore an amber necklace and a silver bracelet around
her wrist. When she told stories, the pure milk-
white of her face would merge with a redness like
the twilight. Her tattoo would widen and the kohl
on her shining eyes would flow with the abundant
generosity of the Bedouin women . . . "Once upon
a time, there was a king and queen, Once upon a
time, there was a boy and girl, there was a camel
driver who wandered Allah's wide earth."

"Mouha, why are you always wandering?"

She pricked up her ears at the low thud that came
to her from over the sand . . . oooh-oooooooooh.

"Mouha, what's that?"

"There was a wolf howling in the desert, and there was a star whose destiny it was to stay up all night." She drew her headscarf over her face and ran away. The amber necklace dangled between her plaits. She rubbed it, and a color like that of the sun diffused from the beads.

"Mouha, why are you always moving on?"

"The mountains are high, the sun is high, the star is high, and the little bird has two wings."

"Mouha, can I run away with you?" We ran away; and there, upon a pile of sand, upon a scented hill with the faint smell of grass, she wandered.

The tents were pitched in a hollow between the dunes. The tops of their poles swayed in the wind. The little girls ran behind them and tripped over their flat feet in the sand. Mouha's scarf hung down the back of her neck and was folded into a little pocket like a pouch. She threw everything into it; her spindle, the twisted woolen braids, dates, and old cigarette ends. When she ran, she lifted up the hem of her embroidered dress and tucked it into the red belt that was tied round her waist. She ran away from me across the open sand, following the herd of goats. The little girls ran with her and then spread out to enclose the herd on all sides. The donkey struggled to keep up under the weight of his saddlebags. The sand stretched forever, tinged with the color of a youthful sun, and their faces drank up the gold poured over the heavens and the earth. They ran and caught yellow scorpions in their lairs. They crushed their tails and the poison ran over the sand. They laughed as they went after lizards. One of the girls found a brightly colored snake in the hollow. She rubbed its mouth in the sand and then pulled out her needle, stitched up its mouth, and left it to writhe in the sand.

"Mouha, I'm exhausted trying to keep up with you. How long will you keep on wandering?"

She laughed, but she didn't turn to look at me. She laughed, and as night began to fall, they gathered on piles of straw amid the ragged tents and began to spin and hum their songs. The fires gave out the same glow as the sun among the domes. The girls who always followed her were sitting in a circle around her. She paid one of them a copper piaster, and the girl turned to her with the needle and drew Mouha's chin nearer to the light of the fire. She pierced the skin with the point of the needle and blood poured forth. The girls went on with their slow rhythmic clapping, and sang:

> *On your chin is a green tattoo, a delight for the*
> *   eye to see,*
> *On your chin is a green tattoo, a delight for the*
> *   eye to see,*
> *Ooooooh-ooooooooooooooooh.*

The blood flowed and covered the bottom of her chin. I was tied to the leg of the wooden bed. I was writhing about in frustration and howling with tears like Mouha's puppy, which used to lick her feet while she undid the cigarette ends and rolled up the tobacco. She blew smoke out of her nostrils, and

the little bird tattooed on her chin shimmered and
flapped its wings and flew away into the night with
the rising smoke. I pulled up my legs and went
back.

Safiya was all over the house, from the pantry to
the courtyard, droning like a bee. Fouz and Rihana
were huddled together, getting on with their
embroidery. If only I'd known what they were
saying I would have told it to Mouha so that she
would play with me, and so that she would know
that I could tell stories too. When I couldn't find
anything to do I went and sat next to Sardoub. The
smell of the bread teased my hunger.

"Should I bake you a dough man?" Sardoub
asked as she flattened the dough, then threw it on
the embers to bake. Then she crumbled a piece of
bread into some milk. I picked it up, walked over to
her room and slowly opened the door:

"Are you asleep, Mother? Are you asleep?" She
didn't answer and I jumped up beside her and some
of the milk spilled. I crossed my legs and some
more milk spilled. I crossed my legs again and
started to eat. She raised her head and looked
toward me.

"Are you sleepy, Mother?" She didn't answer
but I saw her swollen eyes staring at me. "Why are
you crying?" I asked, and her weeping turned into a
violent sobbing. I jumped down off the bed as
quickly as I had jumped up and closed the door
behind me.

I sat outside the house leaning against the mud
step. In front of me was the main gate, massive and

high. On top of the wall over the gate were three
low piles of mud in which poles had been set.and at
the end of each pole a flag fluttered in the wind. I
devoured the chunks of bread while Asaf the dog
walked to and fro. He stopped in front of me and I
threw him a crust. He loitered a while and then
began to dig furiously with his paw under the
bottom of the gate. "Do you want to get out as well,
Asaf? Do you want to run through the fields and
pick grass like Sasa, or run across the desert like
Mouha?" He went on digging and then came back
over to me. He wagged his tail and I stroked his
head and fed him the rest of the bread.

Chapter Two

Guests, be greeted, feel at home,
Pass the coffeepot round to the right.
Leave it there between us both,
Until dawn's star lights up the night.

As the sun started to disappear I felt sorry for myself. Safiya lit the feeble oil lamps in each of the rooms. I climbed up the wrought iron on the window until I reached the drawing of the ghost and looked out at the sky, calm and moonlit, and the pale night. Safiya nudged open my mother's door, then hesitated for a moment before looking in at her body, which lay motionless on the bed in the darkness. I peered out and looked around. All I could see was the high wall on every side, and the grainstores, small mounds of earth along the inside of the wall like endless domes, large and small. The pigeon tower was slightly taller, but even it did not extend to the full height of the wall. I wondered to myself how it might be possible to climb over it. I gazed at the emptiness and the land and the stillness and climbed back down.

Sardoub dragged her mattress out onto the verandah and sat down. Only at night could they creep to her side and sit there. Despite the locked gate and the high wall, in the darkness the girls could come together and talk while she sang them songs and told me stories. Fouz and Rihana sat together and laughed as Sasa gossiped about the market and the farm girls, who had got married, who had had babies, and who had been behaving in a loose way. Safiya, gesticulating wildly with her hands, interrupted the din of the stories: "Enough girl, enough! If she hears you, she'll have you trussed up and thrown in the stables."

And they would interrupt her: "Let the old bitch go to hell. What are you afraid of?" And Sardoub carried on with her song and the girls laughed to hide their fear:

My mind is confused, how to describe you,
You're like a bird in flight, your face is so pretty,
I want to tell the whole world about you,
Tell about the one I've seen, who's so dear to me,
*   my desire, pretty as a picture.*

After that I laid my head on her folded leg, and her warm hand stroked my hair as she told the story of Na'sh: "Na'sh loved his daughters with an insane passion. Seven moons in a black sky they were, and the Virgin fled with her newborn child from the cave where they had hidden, into the vast trackless desert."

I closed my eyes, but sleep would not come. In fact I became more restless. From underneath the mosquito net I watched the open window. Above it crouched the ghost, a drawing in the plaster of a round head and two long arms embracing the top of the window and enveloping my body. At first I used to be afraid. I was afraid of the darkness and the silence and the lizards that I saw during the day behind the grainstores, licking their lips ravenously and disappearing into the cracks. I was afraid of Asaf's barking and howling and the croaking of the frogs which came from the fields far behind the house. But sleeplessness eats fear, and sleep is full of nightmares, and the darkness is a cloak.

I crept out of bed, but this time it was not to go and bury myself in Sardoub's embrace. I wanted to go out. The locked main gate stood before me and the grainstores lay all around. Emptiness and silence surrounded the whole place.

I looked at the sky and sat down on the step. The dew was falling. The Virgin neared the horizon, throbbing she flashed and shied away. Her newborn child, the small star, followed her. Nearer and nearer they came and then faded. Suheil shone in his distant orbit. I could hear cats meowing and Asaf barking wildly. I went back inside and closed the door gently behind me. I went to her room. Would it be silent or filled with sobbing? She was crying. Even in the darkness she cried. Night and day did not exist for her, only darkness and sobbing and then complete silence. I went back to bed. As I lay under the net I listened to Safiya's breathing and pictured her plump, round face, full of kindness.

In the morning I opened my eyes. Safiya was listing off the things she wanted from the market. Sasa's ear, with its green pearl earring, twitched as if to signal she had understood. Safiya repeated the list and I joined in: sweet candy, and sugar strands. Sasa shoved the money into her pocket and I watched her as she saddled the mule.

She dusted off the saddlebags and looked for a short stick to prod the animal with. Then she mounted and her legs, in their trousers with frilly hems, dangled down from under her brightly patterned dress, which she had tucked up. Then she held onto her two pigtails that had been fashioned from Mouha's wool, one on the right and one on the left, with the headscarf in the middle. One of the guards led her clumsily toward the gate as I shouted out the orders once again: "Sweet candy and sugar strands!"

And Sasa replied: "Yes, mistress, yes." She opened her mouth and let out a meaningless laugh; then opened the small narrow door, and the mule trotted off with Sasa bouncing about on its back. I moved from tree to tree, watching her as she shook her pigtails and laughed ecstatically. I detested the wall and the rooms and the main gate with its bolts and latches.

Asaf was chasing the cat, which had come to have a look around the storerooms. She made her escape through the branches, with him hot on her heels amid a racket of barking and meowing. Then he started to dig under the bottom of the gate.

"How long are you going to keep digging for?"

He continued to dig for a little while longer, then he put his head into the hole, bent his back and disappeared. Outside he barked a couple of barks and then he came back in through the hole.

"You've managed to get out at last," I said. I raced over to the hole and put my head inside. It was too narrow. I tried to put my legs through, but I couldn't. I dug at the earth with my fingernails and contorted my feet, but all I got were scratches on my legs and Safiya's screaming in my ears. "By God, I'll tell her . . . she'll know how to deal with you."

I stuck my tongue out at her and ran off. I climbed up the tree again and looked out over the wall. The slave was leading her horse, and the two lads were pulling the donkey. My heart sank. Sardoub and Umm Sasa ran to pull back the bolt. I reached out for the next branch, but my hand missed. The earth spun around me. When I came to, Sardoub was bent over my swollen leg. She dipped her fingers in oil and massaged while curses came flying from every direction.

"I told him a house without a man's like an oasis without a well . . . Miserable little wretch . . . I hope she breaks her neck and her head falls over and knocks against her chest . . . May the good Lord give me the strength and patience to bear what trials and tribulations that son of mine has fathered."

Sardoub interrupted her: "She's only little, mistress," she said, as she dipped the bandages in flour paste so they would bind together and then wrapped them round my leg. Wrapped and wrapped until the world went round and round, and everything started to spin. Grandmother's gleaming teeth moved near and then retreated again, and my heart fluttered from exhaustion. Safiya came and rescued me. She picked me up in her arms and carried me to my bed.

I heard the old woman's curses die down a little, and I waited for her to go. But she didn't go. Instead she poked her nose into every store and box she could find. When she came to Safiya's things, she said: "Why haven't these clothes been sewn? Do you think we get them just to leave them lying here like this?"

She threw them on the floor. Day and night would be miserable as long as she stayed. I crawled about, dragging my bad leg behind me. During the day I saw the main gate wide open and I crawled over to get a better look. Now I could see everything clearly. There was a wider, larger doorway facing ours, and men were coming and going between the two worlds. I could also see small, covered rooms, made of mud, from which smoke was pouring. "When will he come back?" I asked myself.

I heard Grandmother Hakima's footsteps coming and crawled off in the opposite direction. She went and opened the door of his room. No one else would ever dare do such a thing, even when he was away. She lay down on his bed. When she took off her man's cloak and her gold belt, she looked lighter, but she was also frailer and skinnier. She would have the place of honor at the gathering on the long verandah with its wooden railing. Sasa would bring her cushions and she would lean her back against one and rest her arm on another.

Some camels were driven through the main gate, and the mud-domed grainstores were broken open. A line of small girls were loading up the grain and she walked toward them, yelling:

"God curse the faces of your parents! Filthy peasant women, have you no modesty?" And so she would go on, shouting at one or another: "Watch your hand, you filthy thing! . . . Stand up straight, you filthy girl, before I straighten your neck under the sole of my shoe!"

They filled the sacks as I crept from window to window. I couldn't jump or climb, so, dragging my leg behind me, I crawled back, and from behind the edge of the half-open door, where Grandmother couldn't see me, I observed the gathering. One by one the peasant girls came up, each supple young body leaning gently forward while the laborer placed a sack upon her head.

"Dawn's here and I haven't slept a wink," they sang, as another sack gently bent another head. The grain was poured into the gaping mouths of the sacks and the girls exchanged stifled laughs and sighs. "Dawn's here and I haven't slept a wink."

Grandmother Hakima spat on the floor and shouted: "You filthy thing, you earthworm! When will you wash your faces with some shame? . . .

You! You little whore, hurry up, before I take my shoe off in your open gob."

The girls laughed quietly. Why were they not afraid of her? The kneeling camel was loaded up and the pile of sacks bulged out underneath the crisscrossing ropes. The animal rose to its feet while the girls continued their gentle bending and another load was got ready. Afterward the main gate would remain open and many old women would come to join the gathering.

Slaves led the mounts of the gray-haired women wrapped in their black shawls. When they uncovered their tattooed faces their silver-capped teeth shone and heavy perfumes floated out. Their belts were covered in gold, and fat silver bracelets showed beneath the hems of their wide sleeves. She was at the center of the gathering, on top of her pillows, laughing with delight.

"What exactly is going on?"

"No one knows."

The jeweler came in, two weary eyes protruding from behind the thick lenses of his glasses. He wore trousers like the city gentlemen and a dirty fez. He was so skinny that people would have started to laugh, but the minute he undid his bundle and took out his round coins and gold disks and started to punch holes in them, they no longer paid any attention to his appearance. She summoned Fouz and Safiya by name, without adding any of her curses or unsavory expressions. I wondered if they

had just become the offspring of decent folk rather
than that "wretched bunch" to which me and
Rihana still belonged.

Grandmother Hakima measured each one's waist
with a piece of material, which she gave to the
jeweler. He took out a long strap of leather from
which he cut two lengths, one the size of each girl's
waist, and then attached some disks to each. The
next time we saw him, rows of decorated disks
would be hanging among coins, and the jeweler
would open another bundle and take out necklaces
and bracelets and Sardoub would go on singing
about them all night.

> *You with the big silver bracelet on your hand,*
> *And beautiful bangles.*

I asked her why Rihana and I hadn't gotten
anything.

"You aren't the ones getting married. When you
have a figure to talk about, and we can tell your
waist from your chest, then we'll punch some gold
disks for you." She laughed, and the gold disk
hanging from her nose shook in the air.

I wasn't paying much attention to what was
happening. The important thing was that the main
gate was left wide open and every day the jeweler
brought a new bag of wares. And, what was more,
the farm girls, whom I had seen before only in the
distance, were coming in, carrying loads of cotton in
the skirts of their galabiyas which made their bellies

look swollen and which they would throw onto the mat before they sat down.

She was pointing with her stick. "There, put it there. Now, be off with you, you filthy girl! Get out of the way, you piece of dung!"

The girls went off and the women wrapped in black laughed. They twisted the wool into strands with their saliva and made three piles, a dark pile, a white pile, and a pile for the dyed wool. The threads were woven into star shapes and triangles with sharp edges. Sardoub soaked the wool and washed it and unraveled it. Then she would gather it up ready for spinning. Coffee followed coffee, and the smell of ground cardamom floated from the small, thin china cups.

I crawled from room to room and the wooden floorboards scratched my skin and left marks on my legs.

He came, unwrapping his cloak as she ran to hug him. I watched the camels all covered in dust, made to kneel and then tethered. It was the first time I had seen them through the open gate. I could hear the horses' hooves prancing and the slaves dragging their loads. The goat-hair tent was thrown down from the back of the camel and they started to hammer in the pegs. In minutes the tent would rise into the air, wide and spacious, filling the emptiness opposite the gate. All its compartments would be filled with guests. The slaves would come and go, and a large number of peasants would turn up in their faded galabiyas and their flat feet. They would hurry up to him and bow their heads; then they would touch the tips of his fingers and, in an act of submission filled with supplications, they would kiss and kiss, and he, with his head held high, seemed not to heed them at all. When all the commotion died down, he would enter the house, with the slaves bringing the baggage behind him.

He would find her lounging on the verandah, surrounded by the old women wrapped in black with shining gold ornaments dangling from their noses. He would sink to his knees and kiss their wrinkled hands ... and from maternal aunt to paternal aunt his genuflection would continue. He entered the house and Safiya was the first to rush up to him, while I crawled along, my leg wrapped in rags. He picked me up in his arms. "My gazelle, what's the matter? Fatima, Fatima, my little thing."

Grandmother came in with her crooked back. "She's a damned nuisance, climbing up the walls till she cripples herself ... only one leg. By God, I'd break your other leg if it would teach you some shame, damn you."

I muttered: "Sasa ... the souk ... the tree."

He patted me on the cheek. "Fatima my dear, you wouldn't annoy your grandmother, would you? Fatim is a princess. Would you like to be like one of the Turkish princesses, ya-Fatim? You would draw the train of your dress behind you and all the people would bow their heads to beautiful Princess Fatim. And if the King of Egypt himself came to ask for your hand in marriage, I'd chase

him away like a dog. Fatim comes from a long line
of noble folk. She can't marry a Circassian . . . She's
a pure Adnanian filly . . . Off with you, you red-
faced Turk! . . . Isn't that right, my little princess?"

I touched his face. "I'll stay with you. I won't
marry anyone else."

He laughed and laughed from a heart full of joy,
then he put me down and sat down beside me. He
took off his *igaal* and he looked younger, and put
up the ends of his white headcloth on top of his
head. He sat before her as she rubbed her prayer
beads between her fingers. "Did you go east or
west?"

"West."

"And how are things with your father's kin?"

"Drought. Their pastures are dried up and the
summer sun has scorched the land. Half their flocks
are lost."

"Was it the old animals that died?"

"And the young ones too."

"There is no power except in God, may He
compensate us, and them. What have they done?"

"They went east to the grazing lands of Bani
Awna, it's brushland, and there is pasture there."

"Was it peace or war?"

"It will be a year before the drought ends. There
were a few skirmishes, then they agreed not to dig a
well and not to plant palms. One year, and after that
they'll take up their stuff and move on."

"What about your sheep?"

"The Ma'aaza tribe never suffer any harm."

"Your crops are ready for harvesting."

"It's time to gather them in."

"The grain is ripe, and those filthy peasants, they would steal the kohl from your eyes. And those girls that you brought into the world to torment me, someone came to ask for them while you were away hiding in the mountains."

"They're still young."

"Bind them in chains of iron, and throw them into a kind man's house."

"Who came?"

"The Megalli family: Menazi', and his boy, Nayif."

"Who do they want? Menazi'? His teeth have fallen out!"

"Bury them, before they bury your reputation and your fine qualities."

"Safiya?"

"And Fouz, the boy and his father."

"Did you answer their question?"

"Does such a question have an answer? ... Bind them in chains of iron and throw them into a kind man's house. By God, a house with all these calamities in it is an evil omen. Put the dusty bird to flight and then God will give you a son to succeed you, my son."

He fell into a silence. He sipped his coffee slowly, then went out. She returned to the old women wrapped in black. They went back to their work, and their silver teeth shone as they laughed. The peasant women in their colorful galabiyas had tied their black scarves over their foreheads and their plaits swayed against the tops of their breasts,

which could be seen at the open necks of their
dresses. They went through clumps of cotton, each
one sorting and throwing the seeds away. Their
heads swayed as they worked, and they laughed as
they started singing again:

Half my nights I'm out, walking with the moon,
Half my nights I'm out, walking with the moon.
Fetch inkpot and pen, and write on my headscarf,
A young Mamluk took my mind out of my head.
Half of my nights I'm . . .

Amidst the laughter their heads drew together as
they sang quietly. Sardoub came out, and her ample
flesh wobbled as she walked with her stick. She
shouted in encouragement: "Let's hear you sing.
Sing, you pretty things . . . soon we'll be celebrating
your weddings."

They swayed and their faces glowed. They
looked around slyly until Grandmother Hakima ran
into the house with her crooked, skinny body and
was busy poking her stick into the clothes and the
pieces of soap, and the kohl that was being ground,
and the dough that was being kneaded. As soon as
she had disappeared, the rhythm came through loud
and clear:

Dawn's here and I haven't slept a wink.
Dawn's here and I haven't slept a wink.
You, lady, stood behind the door,
Answer me, and be my bride.
She gave me a quarter of an answer

And I turned over on my pillow
And tears of love flowed.

She came out, and her stiff, wooden body walked sternly over to them: "Shut up . . . shut up, you impudent women!" She lashed out at them with her hand. "Quiet the lot of you! Whores, have you no shame? Peasants, sluts, you're a disgrace."

They were standing by the main gate. Sardoub tottered over, leaning her flabby body on her stick: "Never mind, mistress, it's a wedding . . . may God bring joy to your home."

"Such words aren't fit for the stables. Animals! Sluts!"

"They'll sing another song. May God bring joy to your home, mistress."

She turned her back and went back inside the house. Sardoub turned to them and put her finger to her lips: "Sing something decent this time, girls. By God, if she hears any nonsense, she'll have you all flogged."

They went back to sorting the cotton. They were silent and didn't even exchange smiles, each one looking down into her own lap. Sardoub tried to get them going again:

"Sing, sing . . . 'Why, my little birds, do you land where the hunter can see you?'" She clapped her hands in encouragement: "Why, my little birds, do you land where the hunter can see you?"

Chapter Three

We spend all the night confused
At the scattered destinies of our thoughts.
My mind has withered from the effort,
So be kind to me.

Night swallowed up the day's commotion and the moon shone down. The frogs croaking in the nearby fields scratched the silence. I crawled with my bandaged leg to the stone steps at the front of the house and listened to her breathing. The door creaked and I heard his footsteps heading toward her room. I pulled my leg out of the way. Sardoub was snoring in the darkness. I moved closer to her door, but I didn't dare push it open. I just heard the sighs in her voice, which was hoarse with tears. I went back and embraced Safiya's sleepy face. She was dreaming quietly and the rhythm of her heartbeat and her breathing were welcome reassurance. But I soon became restless and I crawled back into the corridor. I heard him leaving her room. He was barefoot, and he was not wearing his *igaal*, and it was the first time I had seen his uncovered head and his thin body without cloak or trousers. I remained silent as he rushed toward the door. I saw him look around, and then the door creaked as he went out. A few moments later I heard the bolt of the main gate. From inside her room came another, muffled, sound which turned into a terrible inconsolable sobbing. I tried to crawl away, but my leg was buried in bandages, and however far I crawled the sound of her sobbing followed me.

"He strangles her," Sasa told me. She had seen him strangle her before. He used to lie on top of her and put his hands round her neck. Sasa was undoing her thin plaits and her face went pale and she shivered. Then she told me that my mother would make those sighs I had heard last night, and sometimes, if she and Safiya took the water jug into her room in the morning, they would find on her neck dark lines that were blue like the thin shadowy veins on her swollen eyelids. They might also see on her dress or on her bed a patch of dried blood.

At first I didn't believe Sasa, however much she insisted it was true. I couldn't understand why he would strangle her when she was so meek and sad and never stopped crying, and when he embraced me he would say: "Ya-Fatim, my little darling, if the dust held off it would be clear."

I loved him and loved him, and I would ask: "What would?"

And he would say: "The sky, ya-Fatim, the sky."

I loved him more. I loved his silence, when he was lost deep in thought. I crawled outside, and her sobbing followed me onto the verandah and down the steps. I was afraid of the night, but her sobbing frightened me more and I wondered why he strangled her.

Asaf spotted me and lowered his eyes. I crawled. Khayra was sleeping in her stable; if I went too close, would she whinny? I crawled on. I felt the thorns against my legs and the blood perhaps drying on the bandages. I crawled. The moon was trying to complete a full circle. The well was just ahead, round like the edge of a full moon, and wide; the steps carved in the rock wound down into total blackness. A few drops of water sparkled in the bottom. I went down, crawling from step to step. The moon's light was pale, and tiny creatures, crawling like me, moved between the cracks and crevices and spoiled the stillness of the water, and the meager light danced on its rippled surface.

"Zahwa, Zahwa, come here. Come take my hand and lead me to the sand dunes far away." The sun was scorching hot, and the dust caked my throat so that I could hardly breathe.

Zahwa was laughing.

"Zahwa, what are you laughing at?" Her laughter rang out even louder as my feet sank into the soft sand and I struggled to move them forward, while she stepped lightly and ran across the sand without her feet leaving a single trace. I ran behind her until the sun waned a little and the crests of the palm trees came into view. She said: "We've arrived."

Seven palm trees stood around the place on every side, and in the middle was a well like the well at our house, round and with steps winding down to the bottom. Even the carvings on its walls, and the cracks and crevices, were the same. This well, however, was full.

Musallam was leaning his head against one of the palm trees, the ashes of a dead fire by his side. His camel grazed sleepily behind the palm trees like a little hill, chewing green mountain mosses. The wind whistled as Sigeema flattened the bread and cooked it on the embers. Zahwa grabbed my hand, "Come over here," and we sat down in front of Sigeema. She was very small, like a child that had been surprised by wrinkles; she looked hard into our faces with her own ruddy face, and tattooed birds and roses and lions cavorted about her wrists. She went on flattening the bread and blowing on the coals. The pupils of her eyes shone with an intense brightness. I ran, with Zahwa, over to the milk churn, and we sat down. The clay pot hung from a rope between two poles.

I watched the tethered falcon with her trussed-up wings. Musallam was feeding her a small bird he had killed. The falcon's eyes were open now, shining like lost pearls, but her wings wouldn't move and the sky was far away. I sensed fear, but with Zahwa pulling my hand I couldn't resist. I would go wherever she went. Musallam was getting his slingshot ready. He had seen a rabbit hopping along in the distance. The wrinkles around his eyes bunched up. He didn't look at us, just followed the rabbit as it leapt about in between the sand dunes. He pulled back the string, but he missed and the stone fell among the sharp stones and the rabbit got away.

Zahwa teased him: "Ya-Musallam, tell us a story, ya-Musallam . . . You've been ignoring your Zahwa for many nights now."

He told a story: "The camels, after they got tired of eating the desert thorns, their humps shriveled up, and they suddenly hated the hobble and the halter. They became stubborn and they screamed and snorted like a storm and no one could stop their madness."

He repeated the story until we were bored with it. Sleep pursued me. Zahwa's face seemed far away and Musallam's voice an echo. The wind whistled like a bee buzzing in my ear, and the light, as it shone down into the well, carried the din of their footsteps toward me.

"Fatim, Fattoum."

"Where've you gone, you miserable bastard? Will we never get any peace from this woeful brood, my son?"

"Fatim, Fattoum, where are you hiding? Your leg, ya-Fattoum, is still injured. Who's upset you, sweetheart?" Sardoub's voice was soft and sympathetic. Then the old woman's ranting and raving came into my drowsy head: "Fatima, girl, what are you doing you devil, sleeping in the well? She's crippled and now she's possessed. There'll be trouble, my son, mark my word. Crippled and possessed, hobbling round the house in the middle of the night, and sleeping in haunted cracks at the bottom of the well. May the good Lord preserve us!" Grandmother Hakima's voice was always accompanied by curses directed at my father's ill-omened offspring, but this was the first time I had heard her say, "May the good Lord preserve us!" At last there was something to frighten her with. I opened my reddened eyes from their restless slumber and glared insolently into her face.

She retreated a step or two. "What's the matter, my daughter . . . Good Lord preserve us and protect us!"

I rubbed my eyes and they grew redder and more alert, but I didn't reply. I just enjoyed her muttered supplications and her retreating steps. "They've possessed her, they've possessed her. May the good Lord preserve us." She turned tail and hurried away.

I buried my head in Sardoub's lap: "I was with Zahwa, ya-Mama Sardoub." I was with Zahwa.

Sardoub caressed me with her warm hand and undid my plaits and ran her fingers tenderly through my hair. "Sleep, ya-Fattoum, sleep. You had Sardoub all worried about you. Sleep, ya-Fattoum, shhhhh-shhhhh."

Safiya went about the house, sprinkling sugar dissolved in water. "Say: I seek refuge in the Lord of the Daybreak . . . Who's this Zahwa she keeps going on about, ya-Sadoub . . . That gazelle she had which died?"

She sprinkled the water and muttered to herself, "What shall I do? Dear Lord, who's going to look after them? What am I supposed to do with them,

Grandmother? The little one and her mother, God knows what will happen to them and all you can think about is grinding kohl and punching gold disks." She wept more, and the *shanaaf* in her fine nose shook and more weeping poured from her nostrils. Whenever the moon was full, the din grew louder and the sobbing increased.

Chapter Four

*The sun hasn't taught me anything
And the moon has been mean.*

She was a pale woman despite all the myths about her. I neither loved nor hated her, but I became attached to her because she was my only way out. Ever since the day she set eyes on Khayra's jet black mane and pure white coat she had spoken that same word 'biyuti-ful.'

My father said: "She's Fatim's filly, belongs to Father's little darling. I can't sell her. Choose any other horse you like." I put my arms round Khayra's neck as she stretched over me and shook her mane, and then she licked me as I looked up from the floor and said: "Khayra's my filly."

She smiled and then noticed my leg and the bandages. At last she became aware of my existence in spite of the fact that she had been into all the rooms and carefully perused everything with those sharp blue eyes. She had taken two white pearl necklaces out of her bag and laughed as she said, "For the pretty little girl." The way she mispronounced the letters made us laugh and

Sardoub hid her face. Safiya closed the door to my
mother's room and looked sternly at the woman.
She didn't want her to see inside. And now the
woman was bending over me examining my wound
with her rough thin fingers until finally she
exclaimed: "No, no, ya-Sheikh al-Arab, she needs
treatment. Her leg is inflamed ... inflamed." The
way she said the word 'inflamed' was unexpectedly
classical and I laughed out loud.

She tugged the end of my plait and said: "Send
her with me. I'll look after her."

Then she looked at me: "Ha, my little dear, will
you give me your beautiful filly so I can train her?"

I said defiantly: "No, she's my filly."

My stubbornness pleased him and he laughed
from the heart and then said: "Fatim, sweetheart, I
could never make you angry."

He turned to the woman and went on: "Fatim is
going to be a princess. A princess like the fair-
skinned Circassian. She's a pure Adnanian, so
doesn't she have more right than any of the other
girls if she is descended from such noble
ancestors?"

She nodded her head as if she had understood
the reasons for his enthusiasm, and my being a
princess, but I don't think she could understand
anything beyond wanting to possess some pure
Arabian breeding stock. "A pure Arabian filly," she
said, and she held the nose, counted and checked
the vertebrae, and inspected the legs, then wiped off
her sweat in delight. And I stared at her more
defiantly and more stubbornly: "Khayra's my filly."

At first I used to call her the Khawagaaya until she told me: "Anne, say Anne." I got to know her house and it remained the only place whose door was always open to me. The guard would lead my filly, with me bouncing about on her back and Sasa running along behind. The more I scrutinized Anne's face the more I realized that she was not beautiful, despite her white skin and her blue eyes and blond hair. No, she definitely wasn't beautiful. As I became closer to her I discovered that her white body was full of blotches and lumps especially on her chest which was inflamed and as red as blood. Her blue eyes showed neither brightness nor life. There was only one expression, and it was similar to that of a spider crouching silently in wait of its prey. She had set her heart on Khayra from the beginning, and it was difficult to still her passion in that regard. She would follow me with her eyes, even at the wedding, amid all the noise, she had ignored the commotion and come and stared right in my face. If I was in a good mood she would smile, and if I buried my head in Sardoub's lap she would ask her about me, and if I was off wandering in my own world she would come after me, and her looks would chase me, and I would run away looking desperately for Zahwa. But Zahwa had left me. And then there was Khayra, her breeding, and her training, and the races. Last but not least there was my education, so that I would be fit to bear the title 'princess,' which I was determined to do.

She was my only way out, but her house was lonely and oppressive. Zahwa had disappeared, and Sardoub had abandoned my hair to move to the room by the lemon tree at the far end of the courtyard to keep mother company with her sobbing, which was turning more and more into clearly audible screams.

My leg was stretched out in front of her. She undid the bandages and looked suspiciously at the wound. She didn't look happy. She said: "It needs cleaning. Your leg's broken as well."

I sat naked in the basin and she soaked my whole body. Sasa laughed: I was so thin and my plaits were dripping wet. I told Anne: "If there had been water in the well I wouldn't have gone down, but it was almost dried up. Zahwa lives at the bottom. She's from the underworld. If she crosses over and arrives at the bottom of the well, I find her there." She laughed.

Sasa splashed warm water in my face as I sat between the two of them. They were both naked. Fine fluff covered their bodies that became thick moss where their limbs met. I pointed, afraid and perhaps a little astonished: "What's that?"

They giggled, and I lifted up the cloth that was wrapped around my waist and looked between my legs. There was nothing there, just fluff. They laughed louder and I could hear both their laughs as I moved away. The laughter became screaming, mixed with moans and cries. Then Mouha wet her fingers with saliva and twisted the strands of wool and tugged at Sasa's short frizzy hair and made lots of intertwining little plaits. Her narrow eyes smiled slyly and she was oblivious to my presence or my going, even when I clung to her.

"Take me there with you . . . I might find her, among the dunes, behind the mountain."

She pushed me away violently. "She's from the underworld. She lives in the belly of the earth . . . We don't have the Zahwa you're talking about."

She hitched up her dress and tucked it into her trousers, which smelled of urine and dung and stagnant water, tied her belt and went out. Sasa was splashing my body and I was laughing. Anne came in, carrying bandages. She seemed surprised, as if she had discovered the existence of something special in me. It was the same way she had reacted to Khayra's mane. She rubbed me dry in the towel and then, leaving me naked, she began to apply the moist ointment that always made my wound turn into a mass of burning flame. I screamed and wept and pushed her away with the palm of my hand. My body was so very thin and tiny and she was easily able to grab my arm with her hand and stop me from leaping about. Her bony fingers felt over my body and in her eyes was the spider silence. My body recoiled and with a scream I stopped her.

Even so, after I had put on my clothes, and she had cruelly tightened the bandages, she drew my face toward her own and looked into it. Then she came even closer and said: "Your face is beautiful." Her fingers traced the dimple in my chin with its little tattoo, or beauty spot as Sardoub used to call it, and she smiled. I ran away.

The guard stood waiting while Sasa wandered round the strange house and I crawled about waiting for one of them to pick me up. Anne would insist: "Every day ... change the dressing."

After that it was my plaits that fascinated her. She would undo them and comb them into a 'ponytail.' And in spite of all Sardoub's warnings not to tell her about Zahwa, I couldn't help it. I told her that my father didn't hunt rabbits. He preferred gazelles, which were really houris from paradise who had come to live on earth. Whoever ate their flesh started to crave it even more, and whoever craved their flesh was pursued by a curse, the curse of the desert, for the desert is treacherous and filled with genies.

I went round with her, limping slightly on a crutch. I learned the names of all her lazy cats that lounged on the chairs and tables, and I would gibber after her 'cat' and 'desk,' and when I repeated the words she would applaud and announce every time how intelligent I was and how much I deserved to become a princess. Grandmother's long nose and her crooked stick were forgotten, as were the main gate and all her curses and warnings about bringing shame if it became known I was out in the streets.

My father smiled at Anne and said: "Fatim is a princess. The Khawagaaya is going to teach her to be like a Turkish princess. Fatim is a pure Adnanian filly."

Sardoub said: "She's only young, mistress."

Grandmother Hakima prodded the soil with her fingers and muttered: "If you don't frighten the ewe into respecting the way, then the ewe will go astray."

However, they soon became too worried about the rest of the flock to bother about the ewe, and I would go to Anne's place every afternoon, with the guard leading me and Sasa running along behind. No one dared to look at me, even the children in the narrow alleys. They would stop their laughing and shouting and be silent till I passed.

The long entrance was planted with sasaban trees, like our house, but she cut hers and pruned the tips of the branches so that they were all an identical cone shape. As we came up the path we would see endless trees: poplars and mastic, camphor, acacia, and willow, and an ancient mulberry under which was a stone water jar that dripped into a brass dish. Anne spent most of her time with the horses, in what she called 'al-istabl,' washing this one, feeding that, training others. She said horses were her passion.

She had acquired all kinds of creatures: tortoises which crawled along under their shells, spine-covered hedgehogs, a snake that she kept imprisoned in a tank, and strange-shaped frogs. Then there were the pens covered in chicken wire where she kept the birds, which were of every shape, color, and sound. There was a peacock, an ostrich, a bustard, and even some injured falcons which she did not hood. And in the last of all those rooms was a young gazelle, which I said looked like Zahwa.

My gazelle Zahwa was very beautiful even though she was exhausted. My father chased her in the armored car until she could run no further and had hidden in the folds of sand. He wanted to bring her to me alive so I could rear her. She was only young, but she was lively, and setting falcons or salukis onto her would have meant certain death. The hawk would bury his talons into her neck and thrust his beak, like a knife, right into her eyeball. They said it made the meat halal, and they could take it and eat it. Even the salukis, despite their speed, wouldn't have been able to keep up with her, and so they were chasing her in the armored car. They had almost given up hope of catching her alive and were already loading their guns, but he refused and said: "She's a gift for Fatim." He carried on chasing her till her body gave and she collapsed on the floor in exhaustion. He carried her by her four legs. She was as light as a feather and her eyes were full of tears. She remained exhausted from the running for a whole week. I offered her grass but she refused to eat. I shared Khayra's sugar with her but she didn't want it. I stroked her little body and she looked at me in grief.

All alone, ya-Zahwa, my dear gazelle, and so sad and exhausted. Her eyes never left me. Her face looked like Musallam's Zahwa, or it was as if the same spirit inhabited them both.

I told her so. Her eyes never closed, and never ceased to pour out tears, which shimmered at the edges of her eyelids, then fell out. Grandmother Hakima prodded the trembling body with her stick: "Slaughter it my son. It's almost finished. Make it halal. It's a shame to waste it."

I wept: "Zahwa, my gazelle."

She pointed her stick at me: "Shut up, you demented girl. I don't want to hear a word from you."

I shut up, but it didn't stop me from wailing as the body of my gazelle was strung up on a hook while the servant skinned it and cut it up. Then came the smell of grilling meat.

Then Grandmother Hakima said angrily: "I take refuge in God, its meat is more bitter than colocynth. I take refuge in God."

Sardoub said: "The meat became bitter from the chase."

And she said: "Nonsense. It's from that wretched girl's wailing, may the Lord protect us from her rotten eye."

Zahwa, ya-Zahwa. Your eyes shine in your head, chaste and imploring. Now your head is all I have left. Your eyes never closed, not even when she threw it down the well. They had the same timid look. The head bloated and decayed and worms wandered in, and those ravenous creatures emerged from your eyes and lapped up their brightness, and as I look on, you turn to empty bone at the bottom of the well.

Chapter Five

By God, how the good times fade away,
The bird of death doesn't hover around,
Nor do the heads of young horsemen continue to roll,
In front of the young girls' camel.

Seven nights passed. The moon's thin crescent became a bisected circle, one half still veiled, the other bright and shining. They prepared the riding camels. Sardoub carried me on her legs. Grandmother Hakima was up at the front, with a slave leading her mount. I was behind, with Rihana and Sasa and the servants and guards and the women in their black face masks. We crossed the agricultural land and then came onto a long path through flat sandy desert. Then we met more irrigated land, half of which was cultivated, and the rest left fallow. We passed again through total emptiness until we came at last to a long wall made of mud in the midst of a vast lake of soft sand.

Our mounts surged forward with the slaves driving them on. We reached the high open doorways above which were mud domes with flags set in them. We smelled the horses and heard hands clapping out a rhythm. The women ululated in welcome and the slaves ran with the animals. Grandmother yelled: "You boy, you shameless creature, slow down, take it easy!"

Fires for making coffee glowed in the darkness and the fragrance of cardamom wafted through the night air. More women wrapped in veils thrust their faces out of the tents and let out joyful ululations. We joined them and they kissed her hand. She took her place in the middle of the gathering, smiling happily. Coffee was bubbling on the fire in front of her. Behind the tent flap the young girls were giggling as they stared wide-eyed at the long row of young men in their turbans. I sat on a mat in her section of the tent and listened to their hushed whispering.

"Mazen is gorgeous. His voice is as strong as a howling wolf."

"What's his voice got to do with it. A man is a man if he's tall and broad."

"Talal is more handsome."

"His mother and father don't have enough to feed an ant."

"Determination is what makes a real man."

"And wealth and slaves and high rank."

"Adlan is like a mule grazing where there's no grass. He's clapping his hands and shaking his head like he were the local desert lion."

"He's fair and well built."

"I don't like that sort. Fair and ruddy, like a gypsy dancer."

"His mother's originally from Aleppo."

"That's right, and he has all the faults of someone from Aleppo."

"Sabig is a lion."

"He's asked for Ratiba's daughter's hand."

"When did he do that?"

"He's been asking for her since the day her anklets starting ringing."

"That's a lie, by God. It's just what Ratiba's been saying to keep the boy on his toes, so he won't flag in his quest for her daughter, who's as black as the slaves who live in the marshes."

Their whispering was everywhere. Their eyes peered out from behind the tent flaps and surveyed the scene, the circles gathered around the aromatic coffeepots, the row of young men stood across from us.

Each young woman danced in turn, covered entirely in black, with her black headscarf drawn over her face. Then she would hand over to her sister, who was waiting inside the tent. They laughed and smeared their heels with ash, and rubbed oil onto the palms of their hands. They tightened their belts around their waists and clapped their hands in time to the beat. Ululations echoed joyfully through the air. One of the women sang to welcome the newest dancer:

Welcome, how well dressed you are,
Good-looking daughter of respectable folk.

She came back into the tent and another one went out.

Welcome, noble eyes of a hooded falcon,
Come, you'll be safe here.

The row of dancers twisted back and forth. Young men would have individual dancing bouts with the young women, him teasing her as she danced to his steps, moving back and forth between the sighs in his voice as he sang of his love for her. She would writhe up close enough to feel his breath, and he would suppress his desire to reach out his hand to tug at the end of the veil and uncover the face filled with lust and desire. Then, with sweat pouring down her veil, she would come panting back to the tent and another one would take her turn.

When it was Rihana's turn, Grandmother didn't pull the plaits that hung down her back, or say: "You've caused us a scandal, you miserable creature." She simply smiled. For those faces that were filled with grief she put on an even broader smile. The fires burned until the crack of dawn.

During the night I had gone to sleep in Sardoub's lap, and I watched them with my own eyes as what was left of the night fluttered away. The fires went out and the slaves brought up the animals. Then sleep dispelled the breaking dawn, taking refuge in our heads, which the night's activities had completely drained.

In the morning there would be a new night, when we would leave Fouz and Safiya. They were packing their belongings into boxes and making sure they had everything they needed. She left her door

half open and there was a lot of wailing and loud
sobbing. It was the only thing that kept the silence
company in the whole desolate house despite all the
trappings of the wedding. Even on the night when
they painted the girls' hands and feet with henna she
didn't come out of her room. Safiya went in to see
her and then came out in tears and said to
Grandmother Hakima: "I don't want to get married
or to paint my hands and feet with henna. Leave me
with her."

Grandmother Hakima prodded her in the chest
with her stick and said: "You belong to your man
now, you miserable creature. And since when do
you think you've any say in the matter, you piece of
camel dung! What's the matter with you, you
loathsome girl? You look confused."

Safiya wept bitterly; then she swallowed her tears
and held out her hands and feet to be painted. Fouz
didn't glance once at Mother's half-open door, not
even as she was getting into the wedding howdah.

The smell of henna mixed with mastic and ben
seeped into every corner of the house, and fragrant
oils were rubbed into their hair. Their brightly
colored clothes were splashed with perfume. They
were both wearing gold ornaments—bracelets,
anklets, bangles, and necklaces—which sparkled and
jangled. Fouz's thin back was bent under the weight
of all the jewelry that clattered against her chest and
waist. Safiya looked beautiful and yet sad, as if she
had suddenly grown to a great age. Anne came,
wearing over her trousers a cloak embroidered with
brightly colored patterns, like Grandmother's. She

had her golden hair down, and her face was unblemished, rosy, and shiny, and she looked radiant and beautiful. The women's eyes were still, and they exchanged knowing glances and whispered to each other every time she stood up or sat down. Her eyes were everywhere, soaking up every detail.

The camels and the howdahs had been ready since sunrise. Father came and lifted first one daughter, then the other, up onto the howdahs. Then he went and locked himself into his room. The party of horsemen moved off, followed by the camels and the howdahs and the rest of the group. The camel driver was in a cheerful mood and sang:

If you ululate for me I'll sing you a song to cheer sad hearts.
I know the one who has smitten me. He's fair of face with a fine long neck.

You could hear the clapping of hands and the young men whistling up ahead. Ululations came from those riding camels behind. The slaves followed on foot.

The music of your bracelets ringing,
Like the sound of Christians singing.

The clapping continued, gunshots were fired into the air, and even the peasant women in their open-necked dresses, with dark, uncovered faces, came out of their houses, followed by the little children who looked on, open-mouthed in amazement, without saying a word. The noise crescendoed as we neared our destination.

> *Today you said: It's our wedding.*
> *I'll come, even if I have to walk barefoot.*
> *Pass the coffeepot round to the right.*
> *Greetings to the guests, and the generous host.*

The young men galloped across the sand, racing their horses. They went far ahead and then came back, and the girls watched them from under their veils, whispering to one another as usual. Whistling filled the air.

> *Dear Lord, love's fire consumes us, the lover's*
> *   dark eyes smite us.*

Ululations split the stillness that lay over the sands and reached the mud walls and open gates to be greeted with more ululations and shots fired into the air. It was like a furious battle in the sky and on the earth.

The two houses were very much alike. Both had rooms made of mud, with wooden ceilings and wide verandahs with steps at the sides. There were also rooms for baking and cooking where the walls were blackened with soot. Each house had a spacious yard where animals were kept and a single mastic tree that gave shade to the space in front of the house. All around was empty wilderness where a few tents were set up far apart from one another.

Each tent had its back to the house and looked out on its own patch of wilderness. The women chatted as they devoured piles of meat served on top of pieces of bread soaked in soup.

One said: "Two sisters in one house; at least they'll provide support and company for one another."

And another said: "It's certainly not easy keeping a girl out of harm's way."

Grandmother offered them one of her sermons: "By God, they bring nothing but bad luck! It's a waste to look after them. They're like a piece of merchandise you get ready for someone else. If you keep her she goes fallow and if you sell her you make a loss."

"You're right, Aunt Hakima. We bring them up and sweat blood, and then they end up in someone else's lap."

"May God protect us from the evil they cause! I haven't had one daughter who's lived. People used to ask me: 'Hakima, where do all your daughters go?' and I would say: 'I pray all the time and God is protecting me from their evil.'"

"You're right, Grandmother Hakima, you're right, but all of them dying like that, is it really just God's will, or . . .?"

"God's will, my girl. I've always said my prayers and not one of them survived. And what a struggle it is from the day they come skriking into the world until the Lord takes them away. Look at my son. God has sorely tested him, but he's managed to remain patient."

They smacked their lips with relish, divided up
the pieces of boiled meat, and then carried on with
their gossip. When they had finished they wiped the
remains of the feast from their hands and gathered
up their belongings. The guests started to disperse,
each group heading off in its own direction. There
were fewer of us leaving than had arrived, and our
heads were bent in sadness. Grandmother was
grumbling to herself. She had gotten rid of one half
of the merchandise but she still had the other half
left. Sardoub tried to hold back her tears while the
rest of us sat deep in silence, each one lost in their
own thoughts. When we arrived home the house
was silent. Mother was in her room, drowning in
tears.

Chapter Six

Why, my little birds, do you land where
the hunter can see you?

I went back to climbing trees. Fouz and Safiya's new home was far across the desert. I looked out toward them sometimes, and cried. I went out most on those bleak, dark nights when there are no stars or moonlight. Mother moved into the single room, which stood all alone on the other side of the thorn bushes. It became her refuge.

Sardoub picked up her own things and said: "I'm going to stay with her until God takes me away, or cures her."

Grandmother Hakima prayed: "May He take you and her away in the same night, and that little genie who's always hobbling about after the two of you."

My father gave a loud sigh as Grandmother continued: "This last one was a boy, and by God his blood is on her dress. The bright red blood of a baby boy, like the blood of a slaughtered animal. The rancid blood of this accursed brood."

"It's God's will, mistress. Nothing's in our hands," whispered Sardoub in a voice that was full of surrender.

Grandmother Hakima responded furiously: "God's will or the touch of the Devil. That woman's brought nothing but disaster since the day she came. Every time God gives her a boy, he gets taken away. And she's deranged. I fear for my soul when I see her having those fits. It's an evil omen."

If Safiya had been there, she would have muttered other prayers in her room, and she would have said to Grandmother Hakima, "May God take you and not leave you on this earth another night. May God curse you wherever you set foot. Evil old woman."

Back in the dusty room I asked Sardoub why they died. Every time they were boys they died? She smiled and answered simply: "God's will." I didn't understand, but I surrendered myself to her hands. She undid my plaits and Zahwa came. "You've been gone so long," I said, "Why have you come now?"

She shrugged her shoulders, gave no answer, and sat down next to me. All around us was desert which the sun had transformed into a blazing furnace. I asked her where she had been hiding. She said: "I was bored. Musallam keeps me imprisoned like a genie in a coffeepot. He says the sun is treacherous and the moon is mean."

I told her how I too had been bored, that Anne no longer came to ask about me, that the house was deserted, and that even when I climbed the trees all I could see was mist. When I asked her why she had left me and where she had been, she said: "The camels tired of eating desert shrubs and despised the halter and the hobble and the bridle. They lost their minds and ran away."

Zahwa was sad. The wounded bird was still tied to the peg, but she nodded her head proudly, and her eyes gazed into the unknown. She was unhooded, and her wings were not bound, but she was silent and moved around the peg, pecking at it with her sharp pointed beak. Then she stopped and was still. I saw tears in her eyes. I said to Zahwa: "Play with me, ya-Zahwa. Teach me the line game and how to play *nugla*. Play with . . ."

The slave came, driving home his sheep. He sat down in front of the bird. She was perched on the peg and he pulled at the tether that was fastened round her leg and prodded her with the end of his stick. She screamed into the emptiness and then flew a little, but she bumped into the peg. The slave rolled over on his back in stitches, and the bird recoiled more. Without the hood I could see her bloody eyes. I turned round. There was only emptiness and darkness and no sign of Zahwa.

The next morning it was seven days since the wedding and we loaded up our things and set off to see Safiya and Fouz. We crossed the agricultural land and then the barren land until we came at last to the gate with its flags.

Fouz had blossomed. She was laughing, and her mosquito net smelled of perfume. Safiya hugged me and wept. She remained with her arms round me for a while, patting me on the back and weeping.

"Is your mother well, ya-Fatima?" I didn't answer and she asked again, "What's the matter with your mother, ya-Fatima."

I muttered, "She was screaming, and staggering about. Then she fell over. They wiped blood from between her legs."

Safiya was greatly distressed and said, "She lost the baby?"

"I don't know. She never stops screaming. Sardoub's taken her to the lemon room."

"Is she still bleeding, ya-Fatim?"

"I don't get to see anything. She sleeps there, and Sardoub stays with her."

Safiya continued her sobbing lament, "My poor mother. I never wanted the wedding and the painting with henna. I told them to let me stay with her." She left everything and started to pace up and down, collecting her belongings from her boxes. She kept saying, "My dear mother, you poor thing." She paced up and down again, but I ignored her and went and put my hands through her husband's *igaal*.

"Come here, you little devil. How's your father?" I chuckled and stretched out my hand to take a piece of sugar candy from his waistcoat pocket. He was tall and thin like my father. He always had sweets in his waistcoat pocket and a

white handkerchief which he would spread over his
fingers and make rabbit ears. "The rabbit's in the
desert with his rabbit ears, but the hunter always
gets him, for the winner is the smartest, rabbit ears."
I laughed, and my laughter filled the room.

All I saw of Fouz's husband were his clothes
hanging on the clothes hook. Safiya was now
addressed as 'Aunt' Safiya. I was amused: "When
she lived in her father's house we used to call her
Safsoufa."

She laughed.

"My aunt now has the keys to the storeroom and
the mill."

Safiya continued to pace up and down, collecting
rags. Her husband noticed her tears: "What's the
matter, light of my eye?"

Her weeping turned to uncontrollable sobbing:
"My mother's sick. I must go back to her. There's
no one to look after her, the girls are too young."

Her wailing grew louder and he gave in. "Don't
stay away too long, my dear." She smiled and pulled
me into her arms.

Grandmother Hakima stared at him: "You
ridiculous old man! How can you let your bride go
off like that? Let her mother go to Hell. She's
brought us nothing but grief."

"The girl's still a timid young filly. She needs
careful handling ... In any case, her mother is my
cousin and yours too. She shouldn't be treated like
an outlaw."

Grandmother waved her hand in the air and
continued: "That damned girl has learned how your

mind works. May God curse all women, and may I be the first!"

The girls giggled at one another and Safiya returned home with us. As soon as she arrived, she removed her veil and went straight over to the dusty room. Sweat was pouring from my mother's face. Sardoub mopped her brow with a damp cloth: "She's had this fever since the day of your wedding." Safiya stifled her tears, but Rihana stood in the corner weeping openly. We heard his footsteps approaching and the crying stopped. He came in and Sardoub shooed us away from the bed. Mother looked at him through half-open eyes and dripping sweat. He held her hand and tears poured down from her heavy eyelids and mingled with the sweat. He took off his *igaal* and dried her face with his headcloth. He dried a tear that brimmed in his own eye and then let out that long sigh of his.

He picked me up and carried me out of the room in his arms. The tears were still in his eyes as he said: "Ya-Fatim, separation hangs over all of us, and it is written that each of us must one day go far away." I hardly dared to breathe. Was she dead? He went on: "If only the sky had cleared. When a bird migrates it doesn't come back. It doesn't send letters. When a bird migrates it forgets."

A great silence settled over the house. Sardoub brought her sheepskin rug back from the lemon room. She was silent and grave. All she could do was wail, "Oh my grief, my pain." The drums beat until I even began to detest the sound of water dripping from the stone jars into the dish. The mourning lasted for three days. The women took turns to sing our departed mother's praises. Grandmother slapped her cheeks in grief and wailed with the other women. She had painted her face with black dye.

You were a princess, a daughter of nobles.
You were a flower, a bloom among thorns.
You were a jewel. None was like you.
You were beautiful. Praise be to Him who
  created you.

The echo of the wailing resounded in my ears. I wept and then fell asleep. Zahwa wept with me. She said, "Sorrows should be shared." The genie came with us to the well and we wound our way down the stone steps. The genie laughed and her laughter had a thousand sounds. She revealed her black, crooked body and we looked at the small, hard lumps sticking out of her back. When she laughed you could see one big tooth in her mouth which hid half her tongue. Her body was covered in black hair which looked like spines. She was repulsive. Was she a wolf or a monkey?, I asked myself. I was too afraid to speak. We splashed water on the genie's body. Our hands touched a large stone in the well and we could feel engraved symbols on it. We continued splashing her body, and the echo of her laughter shook the sides of the well. Reptiles and insects hid in the crevices. Her eyes met mine and in them I could see my terrified face. She picked up a sharpened stone and cut me with it just below my eyelid. Blood dripped onto my eyelashes, and I cried. Zahwa wiped the wound with water, and laughed and laughed. The genie laughed too, then drew her cloak around her and left. I felt my wound and then forgot about it as our hands went to work removing the engraved stone. We brought it from the bottom of the well and put it down on the top step. Zahwa said, "They are pharaonic engravings." And she pointed with her finger, "A bird, a flower, a gazelle, they're pharaonic symbols."

We left the well. My eyes were swollen from crying and my wound was bleeding. Zahwa said, "Your mother has gone to live in a new land. Don't be sad."

I was exhausted and I slept. When Sardoub woke me she felt the scar on my eyelid, saying, "Who wounded you, Fatim, who hurt your eye? It's swollen." She picked me up in her arms and patted my back. "Fatim, my dear, you're crying and your heart is broken in two . . . Who hurt you, ya-Fatim?"

I whispered in her ear. Perhaps she would believe me. "The genie is repulsive. She has lumps on her back, and a tail. Yes, really, she has a tail, ya-Mama Sardoub. Zahwa said we should splash water on her, so we did. Then she came out of the water and wounded my eye. She scarred it with a sharp stone and said, 'This is the key of life. Your hair will grow very long, and hang over the clouds while your feet remain rooted in my well. I will protect you with the symbols of Pharaoh. You will never die, and crows will never hover round your plaits.'"

Sardoub patted my back. "Sleep ya-Fatim, my little one. You've started to talk about life and death." And she sang me a lullaby:

Sleep, my dear, and I will plant you a seed,
and set free a pigeon for you,
and punch gold disks for your wedding.

Why wouldn't she believe me? The genie told me it was the key of life, and I saw it with my own eyes, a pharaonic symbol. Why doesn't she believe me? Didn't she herself find the pharaonic stone in our well and say that we should use it for milling the grain?

Safiya's crying became a habit and she covered herself in black. She refused to answer her husband.

"Get home, light of my eye."

"Who can I leave them with? They are still young, and the house is empty. There is no one to protect them or give them affection."

Every time he came back he would bring a bottle of perfume, dresses, and gold jewelry for her to fasten onto her dress. He would whisper to her: "Come home with me, light of my eye," and she would get more annoyed.

"I haven't set foot in this house for over a year. Her blood still hasn't dried in her veins and all you can think about is satisfying your own desires."

Grandmother's appeals only served to strengthen her resolve: "That man of yours is head over heels in love with you, you wicked girl. I tell you, the only thing that will work with you is a stick. Your husband's full of nonsense, and he's still after you. If he was a real man, he would drag you home by the hair."

Safiya answered defiantly, "You expect me to leave them just to find someone else drowning in their own blood the next time round."

Her tongue was becoming more insolent in its responses. Father let out his usual sighs and stared into the distance, well beyond the dunes and the hill and the barren land. Rihana went back to embroidering her clothes in silence. The house was dreary and oppressive, and Anne never asked about me. Even when she heard mother had died she didn't come. My hair grew longer. Every day it grew and grew to the sound of my screams. Safiya would comb it. The nights were long, and all I could see from up the tree was emptiness and desolation. The croaking of the frogs became a drum beating time to my grief.

Chapter Seven

Last night a dream told me,
Good things come to those who wait in patience.

If, as they say, the desert is a sea, then who plunges into its sands? The camels of course. But the camels have been patient for so long, they have eaten desert thorns and their humps have withered. They have become weary and obstinate and seek revenge for the years of hobbling and haltering and tethering.

The smell of dust filled the air, and Sigeema said: "Sandstorm . . . the gazelles are bleating."

They covered their faces and hid their mouths as the silence descended. There was no sound save the whistling of the wind. The wind blew louder, and the eye of the sun was pierced and grew swollen red and then was finally obliterated by the dust. Musallam tightened his headcloth and wrapped his cloak about his shoulders.

The storm grew worse, and Musallam dragged himself into the tent as the sand kicked over everything in its way. They let down the tent flaps and crouched in the far corner. The howling of the

wind seemed to go on forever. At last stillness
came. The stars were obscured by a dark cloud of
dust. Musallam's grim face was deep in thought.
Sigeema sang her songs as she wet her fingers with
saliva and twisted the wool into yarn.

Zahwa spread out my palm and read my fortune:
"There was once a king and queen who only ever
had baby girls. Every time she conceived, and the
king waited for his heir, she would give birth to a
daughter, whom the king would throw into the
palace well."

I told her: "Grandmother Hakima doesn't throw
them into the well; she just strangles them." Like I
saw him strangling my mother. It was she who told
him to kneel on her body and kill her. But every
time he tried, he saw the tears in her eyes and he
would have pity on her and return to his room. Sasa
also saw him strangling her, lots of times. Even
when he locked her in the room she wouldn't die.
The only ones who died were the boys.

Zahwa spoke to me again: "Say a prayer for the
Prophet and hold out your hand."

I spread my palm and she continued her story:
"Each time the king threw a daughter into the well a
small palm tree would grow nearby. In the end
there were seven palms, all bearing clusters of dates.
But no boys came, and the queen wept and made
vows and prayed to the Lord to grant her anything
but the affliction of another daughter. Then she
conceived, and when her labor pains came, her
handmaidens told her that she would have a boy but
that he would live only if no living person, including

herself, were to set eye on him until the time was right."

I said: "If they had hidden the boys from Grandmother's eye, would they have lived?" Safiya used to say that her eye could split stone, and that it was her vicious eye that had done away with them. If only her Lord would take her away, then He would bring us all great relief. But she remained and my mother moved on.

Zahwa was silent. She resented my interrupting her. I urged her to continue: "Then what happened? Ya-Zahwa, what happened? Did the right time come?" She turned her face away and said nothing.

Sigeema sang: "Good things come to those who wait in patience."

I plunged into the dark, dusty, night jumping from tree to tree, looking into the emptiness. Safiya sighed when I started to tell her: "There was once a king and queen who only ever had . . . "

Then she screamed furiously at me and my overactive imagination: "You're chopping my poor liver into pieces. Where do you get such stories? By God, the only thing that's spoiled you, you little bitch, is all the time you've spent with those slaves. What on earth are you doing with the likes of Sasa and Sardoub, and that she-goat Mouha who picks up scraps from the floor and covers herself in sheep droppings? Can't a daughter of noblemen find anyone better than Mouha and Sasa who teach you such ridiculous tales?"

I screamed at her: "Zahwa told me the story. Why won't you believe me? Zahwa, who has two pigtails and who lives at the oasis with Musallam and Sigeema and the little slave. Don't you know them?"

Safiya slapped her cheeks in despair and wailed: "It's the things your eyes have seen that have unbalanced your mind, you poor thing." I felt the sympathy in her voice and made no comment and did not try to convince her of anything.

Rihana was always serious. Since the day Fouz left her she had been embroidering without saying a word or managing a single smile. She didn't seem to care about anything. The number of her cloaks and her bedspreads grew, and she stitched with her colored threads and sewed beads onto every piece of cloth she could lay her hands on, even her slippers and socks.

Every market day Sasa would put her woolen braids in and put on her perfume. She would bring me sugar candy and pieces of sugar, and, for Fouz, thread and needles and mother-of-pearl and beads. Sasa had grown up.

Sardoub said: "There's a fire raging in that girl's slumbering body." Umm Sasa turned to her with fear in her eyes.

Mouha had grown up too. Sometimes she would take the trouble to speak to me or tell me a story. She would let me collect scraps of material for her, and then pat me kindly on the shoulder as if she were Safiya or Sardoub. Mouha had grown up, but she was still mysterious and silent, and her narrow, shining eyes gave nothing away.

Umm Sasa said to Sardoub: "If our masters go out hunting, we can nip it in the bud."

Sardoub said: "Leave the farming to the farmers." Then she continued: "As long as the mind is sound, leave things to the man who'll take her."

Umm Sasa, however, had made up her mind: "She's young, the mind is easily led astray, and no man has appeared. My daughter is still young, Aunt."

Sardoub sighed reluctantly: "She's your daughter and you're the one who must look to her honor."

I asked Sardoub about the bud, but she wouldn't answer. Then I said, as Sasa screamed in the locked room and the blood ran down between her thighs: "It's not fair, Grandmother. Why do they have to pluck her hair? I saw it when she was bathing with Mouha."

She stroked my head so that I would sleep, or go away. "It's hurting her, ya-Mama Sardoub . . . Sasa's going to die. It grew itself. No one planted it there."

When I asked Safiya how hair was planted and why people hid it, she licked her lips and moaned: "It's none of your business, hair and planting and pruning. Go and play somewhere else."

Fouz never came, and Grandmother Hakima's wrinkles moved in on her features and dark blotches appeared. My father didn't come back, and Anne never asked about me.

I started running away again, climbing from tree to tree, besieged in a void. The mud-domed grainstores looked on while restless creatures crawled beneath their walls. Na'sh's daughters were dancing in the sky, with seven spirits, sinking out of view, then reappearing again.

After a long absence the new moon finally appeared. They opened the huge main gate, and Sardoub got to her feet. Young and old alike came running. He was back at last. He came in. His face was more haggard than before, and there were shadows around his eyes. His thin face was caked in dust from the journey. He kissed her hand and embraced me. "Fatim, my little darling, your plaits have grown. I've been away a long time."

He was gentler and more affectionate. Grandmother asked him about comings and goings over her lands, and for news of her maternal and paternal cousins. He answered simply: "All is well."

For a moment he was lost in thought, then Safiya came and kissed his hand. Rihana followed her, but they didn't dare sit down lovingly at his feet like me. Grandmother called Safiya over and looked at him: "How long are you going to let her bring shame on us, abandoning her family and her master?"

Tears shone in Safiya's eyes and he wandered deeper in his own thoughts as he hugged me. Then he said: "Fatima, my dear, tell your grandmother that all the pain has crushed your father."

The anger on her face was mixed with worry, and she did not respond. But she was unable to remain silent for long: "A house without a man is like an oasis without a well, a wasteland. Only a tent peg keeps a tent up, and a tent peg needs ground to hold it. A good woman will provide you fertile pasture, my son, where you can find solace after the desolation you've tasted."

I opened my eyes to watch him. His face was still grave.

Fouz came eventually. Her belly was swollen and her breasts rose and fell as she walked. Her husband didn't come, however. Instead it was his father who appeared, and he was angry. He didn't get any sugar candy out of his waistcoat pocket, nor did he play 'rabbit ears' with me. He spoke sternly to my father:

"Both girls are back in your house. Now, either you give them back, the two of them together, or you keep them here and look after them yourself. I've been patient for a year. I've tried to humor the filly, but she's just grown more headstrong. If you can't keep her under control and you're her father, then how's anyone else supposed to handle her?"

When he had said this, he tossed his coffee away without drinking it. Then he got up to go. "Next month me and my son will be getting married. If it's not to your daughters it will be to someone else's."

Grandmother let out a great wail as he disappeared, and then grabbed Safiya by her hair: "You wretched girl! What will the Arabs say about us now? You said you were coming to mourn. Well, you've slapped your cheeks enough. So help me God, if you don't collect your rags and obey your master and husband, I'll slit your throat like a lamb and string you up on the tent pole, you impudent girl."

Safiya burst into tears once more: "The girls are still small."

Grandmother interrupted her: "We'll get someone to look after them. Don't you trouble yourself about it. By God, no one needs some bringing-up more than you. You're a waste of time."

They exchanged curses, one out loud, the other under her breath, and my father said nothing. He stared into space and then leaned his head on my leg. I began to run my thin fingers softly through his hair. "If only you hadn't strangled her with your own hands. I saw you do it once, and Sasa told me she's seen you do it many times. I had given you pride of place in my affections, and in spite of everything I still love you."

My mind wandered for a moment. When I came to, I saw Fouz and Rihana sitting together. Rihana was smiling at last, and she had laid out in front of Fouz everything she had sewn in her absence. They chatted affectionately and were oblivious to what was going on around them

Safiya was moping about, packing up her belongings and weeping through swollen eyes. A day passed and then another, and on the third day my father loaded them up and took them back to their husbands' house. The same miserable silence returned to our house, even though there was in fact another wedding being held, and another set of merchandise being delivered, as Sardoub put it. Rihana gathered her things and punched her gold disks in silence. There were no ululations, no shots fired into the air, no wedding dress, and Dawwaba, with her thin body and jangling anklets, came to live in our house. Grandmother said: "She's from a good family, and a paternal cousin." Sardoub said: "Only God endures forever, and now she's come to take your mother's place."

The house was empty save for the sound of her footsteps, and the thick heavy anklets full of disks which jingled in the silence. They said she would bring sons, and fill our devastated house with life, and the tent peg would find rest in robust fertile earth. His patience, however, didn't last a week before he was off on his travels once again. "Hunting and shooting," he said.

Grandmother said: "Why are you deserting the new love in your life?"

When she occupied mother's room I was heartbroken. I chose to go and live in the lemon room, sleeping on the same bed that she had died in. Dawwaba threw out mother's mosquito net and rolled up her bedding. Some young women came to do the upholstery and sew the covers and other furnishings. Dawwaba had also brought soothsayers and sand readers and old women who burned incense and recited spells and splashed water on the walls and wrote spells to bring true love. But he didn't return. She read the marks in the sand, and looked everywhere for a sign, and saw auspicious omens every step of the way. Safiya wasn't there to

wail over memories. There were only my tears,
which I shed in abundance and which Sardoub
wiped away with her hand. She said: "You're
starting to understand, ya-Fatima. Your heart has
known sadness, my little one."

I felt as if the house was closing in on me, even
though the room was empty and the familiar sound
of breathing no longer came from the bed. The
body of Sardoub, and Sasa and her mother, always
seemed to get under my feet, and I could no longer
stand the windows and the wall. All I could bear
were the tops of the trees. I climbed them at night
and sometimes dozed off there. I climbed them
during the day and watched life going on around
me. I couldn't stand the house at all. Grandmother's
sight was becoming weaker, and she no longer saw
me or tried to admonish me with her usual curses.
She had decided to grow old quietly.

Dawwaba wandered about the house, busy with
her incense and her spells, while he stayed far away.
His absence grew longer and he did not return. The
old women, dressed in black, said to her: "It looks
like the bird has left his mate."

She didn't answer. Her belly had swelled up and
she was preoccupied. She became so vain that she
no longer bothered about anyone. The house
became more stifling.

I could only find peace of mind up the trees,
among the branches that hung their leaves over the
wall. But sleep overcame me and I fell off the
branch. This time Sardoub scolded me: "Not again,
ya-Fatim." My leg was in agony. Bandages were no

use and they had to fetch somebody to set the bone while I screamed.

Grandmother broke her silence and said: "Didn't I tell you all she was cursed? Demented cripple!"

She had started to call me 'the cripple.' "The cripple went, the cripple got up . . ." Even Dawwaba took a liking to the name, and she called me by it as if it were a pleasant and amusing title.

I could no longer seek shelter in the trees. All I could do was crawl, and sleep was my only refuge. The house, despite all its spacious rooms, seemed cramped, and the noise of Dawwaba's footsteps as she moved about drove me insane. A heavy atmosphere of gloom hung over the place. I wept. Sardoub whispered, "Why are you crying, little one? God will make your leg better, don't be afraid. Young women have a thousand faces. Tomorrow they will hobble about on sticks while you will move gracefully like the moon in all its glory. A girl has seven faces."

I cried a lot as I lay in Sardoub's arms. I told her that I didn't want to stay there, in the lemon room, and that I could no longer stand the house. She caressed my hair with the palms of her hands, and tears welled in her eyes. In the morning Sardoub dragged her rug back over to the room. Sasa dusted the cobwebs out of the corners and filled the cracks in the walls with mud, and sprinkled water on the floor. It was a single room, with a raised verandah and a narrow window, that stood at the far end of the wall, well away from the trees and the thorns and the pigeon tower and the storerooms. It was where my mother had bled and died. Grandmother Hakima had said: "She's deranged, always miscarrying her sons. She shouldn't be living with Muslims, that woman. She's demented. My heart bleeds for you, my son, living with the insane, and you remain patient."

Dawwaba had Mother's bed carried over to me, and her mosquito net, bedspread, mirror, and a chest of clothes. She sent them with Umm Sasa, as if she was relieving herself of a great burden that troubled her and brought her bad luck. She was very happy with my desire to separate myself from the rest of them. Even though I never caused her any annoyance she was still relieved. They all went and Sardoub remained with me. She rubbed my leg. During the day she caressed my hair and at night we sat on the verandah and watched the stars and exchanged silence.

When my father came back, Dawwaba said to him: "Your daughter is mentally unhinged. She talks to herself and climbs trees like a monkey in the middle of the night. She communicates with genies. If she stays near me I'll lose the son in my womb. Your daughter is bad luck. The woman who reads the lines in the sand, all those who read the sand, have told me that there is a black stone in my way. Your daughter is evil. If you're not afraid for the baby, I am. Even her own grandmother never calls her anything but bad luck." She spat down the inside of her dress to ward off any evil that might be hovering, and then carried on: "She has people to serve her. If you want to be with her, go and stay with her. Otherwise I'm going back to my family's house."

He came and sat down next to me and Sardoub, and was silent. It was a moonlit night. He did not pick me up in his arms, nor lean his head against my chest. My leg was stretched out in front of him and I saw a still tear in the corner of his eye. I asked him, "Was it Na'sh who buried his daughters or they who buried him?" He didn't answer.

Sardoub said: "You've grown up, Fatim. You're aware of what's going on. You understand, and you carry your own troubles. Look at her hair." He didn't look or utter a word. He simply stood up and left, solemnly, as he had come.

Zahwa started visiting me regularly again. I would talk to her while Sardoub listened in. Sigeema too looked kindly upon me, and would keep repeating her ditty, which she never changed:

Last night a dream told me,
Good things come to those who wait in patience.

Chapter Eight

Despair and distance and seven wounds,
I'm afraid of them, afraid they'll break my heart.

The soft swells and winding curves of the desert's body shift and change. The sands creep and the floods trace furrows of sadness across the lonely desert tracks. Those raging sandstorms always carried something away. The wind would whistle and howl and then snatch up a filly or a mule, and sometimes whole tents and pastures. Musallam disappeared, even though he knew the desert like the back of his hand. He knew its night sky and its changing moods, where to set up his tent, and when the clouds would be heavy with rain. He had roamed far to the east and west, and spent days and nights alone there. He knew all the wells. Sometimes he would stretch out his wizened old legs, take off his *igaal*, and stories would flow from his lips. He would talk about the tribes, their origins, their territories, and their latest news. No one knew the desert like Musallam.

People often wondered about his tribe and lineage. Some said he was a peasant who longed to live the life of the Arabs but had been despised by them. But then when they heard him reciting the poems of al-Mutanabbi and Ibn al-Roumi, and others whom he had memorized and recited at their gatherings, they were amazed. Some maintained that they spotted in his accent the traces of an Azhar education, of someone who had been to the *kuttab* and spent time as a student at the Azhar. Any doubts about his origins also disappeared when they saw how he pruned and grafted his palm trees, and how strong young trees sprouted up from the shoots. He also knew much more about horses than they did, and was more familiar with the different pedigrees than they were. Stubborn young fillies were his specialty. They would leave the horse with him, and he would tame it and fatten it up and then lead it back meekly to its owner. Then there was his deep knowledge of desert plants, which he would gather and pound and blend and use to cure ailments. So, although they were unable to determine his exact lineage, they could not help but revere him, for besides the wrinkles of age on his cheeks and forehead, his bearing was solemn and dignified, and he was generous. His tent was open to all who passed through. Coffeepots bubbled on his fire, and his food was in every mouth. Moreover, he never crossed anyone, nor envied others for anything they had. If anything, he was more generous than any of them. Take wells for example. They attract shepherds from miles around and are the subject of their quarrels and arguments. Musallam would dig a well and plant his palm trees.

Then, if the shepherds came and set up their tents by his, he would set off into the open desert and disappear for two or three days. Then he would return, load up his tent on his camel and move on to set up a new home. He would tap the ground with the sole of his foot, dig his well, and plant his trees. It was as if he had known the new place all his life, or it had known him.

When asked about it, he would laugh and say: "Wells are like udders. They fill up and they dry up, each one at its own time." Their mouths gaped in astonishment. Had he really explored the whole desert and knew which wells were full and which were empty? Had he lived long enough to learn all this?

When Musallam went off this time, he didn't come back. The sandstorm was a swirl of dust. He disappeared from in front of his tent. They searched everywhere and asked every traveler they saw. Accounts of his disappearance varied, as did accounts of his life. They asked Abou Shreek, who guided the pilgrimage caravans, about him, and stayed up long into the night as he told them the following story:

Musallam had been a prosperous and wealthy man. He owned large tracts of fertile agricultural land by the Nile. He married a Turkish woman called Zata or Laza. Abou Shreek wasn't sure of the exact name. She was very fair-skinned and very well built. When she moved, her body wobbled like a sack of ginned cotton. One day he was passing the house of the local governor, and he saw her combing her hair in the courtyard. Her hair was long and luxuriously soft. He was on his gray mare and he stopped right in front of her. He was so overcome by her white skin and her prettiness that he raised his eyebrows. When she stood up to throw stones and sand at him, she looked like a young girl, though she was full of fury. He married her, and it's said that he gave all he owned for her bride price. After that the woman grew even rounder and more corpulent, and maybe she was a bit tyrannical and boasted to him about her Turkish roots. No one knows exactly what happened between them, but he started to loathe living with her and would love to go off on his own with his tent and his racing camel. He hunted more and made many journeys to the east and west of the desert. But he was by his nature inclined to do this, for he had had no children, neither by her nor by any other woman, and he was not fond of the noise and commotion of household life. Abou Shreek believed that the Turkish woman was still alive, and that she was now old and ugly, still white and plumper than the first sack had been; congested veins stuck out of her white skin like blue lines drawn by age.

Abou Shreek conjectured that Musallam had missed her and longed for her company. That's what he'd said in his final days. Then he'd been silent, and Abou Shreek wasn't entirely convinced: how could he leave Sigeema, his skinny old wife, and Zahwa, his daughter, alone in the wilderness, especially since Sigeema was also his wife? Sigeema

wasn't fair and she didn't weigh anything next to a
sack of cotton or anything else. She was very short
next to him, and dark-skinned, the color of ripe
dates, and extremely thin, and she had tattoos
engraved on her chin and over the palms of her
hands and around her wrists. Her eyes were small,
but they shone brightly with agile energy and when
she opened them wide they radiated kindness and
self-sacrifice.

I wanted to tell Zahwa that my father, too, had
gone away and forgotten about me, that he didn't
love Dawwaba, and that he hated the house, just as
Musallam had left Laza, except that father would
never leave me, never leave Fatim. I didn't even
dare ask her about the king whose son hadn't seen
him, and if it was now time to see him. I didn't open
my mouth, for she was sad and wept. My own eyes
were too swollen to cry, but I laid her head down in
my lap, and my hands, though they were small,
mopped the tears from her cheeks.

I told Sardoub that Musallam had gone away, and
that Abou Shreek said he had gone to Laza. Had my
father also gone to see my mother? Would he come
back?

She didn't answer. She said: "Everyone who goes
away comes back in his own time."

I asked her when it would be time for the king to
see his son whom he hadn't seen yet, but she
remained silent. The croaking of the frogs was the
only sign of life. Sasa came with a small table every
morning and evening, and we would eat. Me and
Sardoub divided the food between us, and

sometimes Mouha would join us. She had started embroidering young men and lions and open roses inside intertwining triangles on my dresses. She told me the story of the gazelle that had three little ones and the wolf that chased them. They hid from him in the white dust of the flour mill, and the mother cut open his belly with her horn to look for them.

Sardoub no longer said anything. Deep in silence she turned the millstone which had the pharaonic carvings on it and ground the cereals. Then she put it in bags, and Sasa carried it over to the storerooms.

Sardoub said: "It's a way to make an honest living."

But that wasn't exactly true, because she would turn the millstone even if there was nothing on it. She would just hold onto the handle and keep turning while her face beamed with joy. I looked at her, but she didn't speak.

When Dawwaba found out, she said: "I said the girl was consorting with genies and you didn't believe me. Whoever lives with her suffers serious damage. She's deranged, I tell you. Whoever goes near her is doomed."

But Sasa didn't stop coming. Neither did Mouha. Sardoub went on turning the millstone and smiling. Sometimes at nights she would hold me in her arms. Khayra refused to eat, so they brought her to me. I felt comforted by her whinnying, and I crawled over and spoke to her: "Khayra, my love, do you want a piece of sugar? Safiya's gone, ya-Khayra, and Fouz and Rihana have gone. Grandmother's just bones and flaps of wrinkled skin. When my leg's

better, Khayra, I'll take you out. I'll open the main
gate and we'll gallop away. Mouha will tell me the
way to Zahwa and we'll escape to her. She's on her
own now, just like me and you."

When my father returned, he came and sat down
next to me. He was soon lost in thought. She had
borne him a daughter. They called her Samawaat.
Sardoub said: "That was your mother's name, God
rest her soul." I didn't know my mother's name
was Samawaat. All I knew was that she was my
mother, with her tearful eyes. At last Anne came.
She stroked Khayra's mane and it seemed like she
had forgotten me. She said to my father: "She's a
pure Arabian filly. If ever you think of selling her,
remember me."

My father looked at me and said: "She's Fatim's
filly."

She realized then that I was there, crawling, and
she laughed. "Not again, ya-Fatim."

I said to her: "This time the wound is very
deep."

She discovered that my hair was almost down to
my knees and she looked carefully at the scar
underneath my eye. She said: "Who put that mark
on you?"

I said: "The ugly genie. I saw her with Zahwa."

She laughed again, and I heard her familiar
chuckle return, and felt her fondness for my words.
"Come, ya-Fatim, come with me. Would you allow
me to borrow your filly, we could train her and
breed from her another beautiful filly, and then I
would give her back to you.

I said, with the stubbornness I had become used to: "I won't leave Khayra. Khayra is my filly." And she answered immediately: "Who said you would have to leave her? I'll take you with her."

Then she looked at my father. "Her leg needs treatment, maybe even surgery. She's still young and there's no one to look after her. I'll educate her. She'll become a princess." She said all this at once. He didn't reply, then he nodded his head, painfully resigned.

Grandmother Hakima came out of her silence to curse me: "You little parasite! Where are you going to leave your father's house for now, you little cripple? I've been praying that we'd get rid of you, may God deliver us from your evil!" She said this as she, too, gathered up her things.

"Two sets of baggage will be leaving," Sardoub said. Grandmother Hakima was getting her belongings ready to join the pilgrimage caravan. She said: "My bones have grown old, 'and the good things that remain are better.'" Her veined hands played with the prayer beads.

Sardoub packed for me all the clothes that Mouha had embroidered. Sasa undid my long braids and they poured water over them. Zahwa came with heavy tears in her eyes. She said: "You're leaving me."

I said: "I'll come back, ya-Zahwa, I'll come back. My leg will get better; I don't want to stay like this, limping everywhere, a cripple."

She was silent, then she took off her necklace and gave it to me. There were seven eyes on it, threaded with blue beads. She said: "Wear it, ya-Fatim. It will ward off evil, and protect you."

I laughed. "Me, Fatim the cripple, bringer of doom. What's going to protect me from my own evil, ya-Zahwa? What will ward it off?"

I cried in Sardoub's lap, and she muttered: "I wonder when the eyes of those who part will meet again."

I buried my head in her lap and continued to sob until Anne came and took me to the car with the covered seats. She pulled me by the plaits. Every time I wandered, she said in her strange accent:

"Come on, Fatim, don't be sad."

I let my eyes roam far away, while the eyes on my necklace wept like open sores on my chest.

Chapter Nine

Many lands lie between us
And my heart is torn in two,
Separated by great distance,
Scorched in a fire of longing for you.

The mansion and all its rooms were lonely, and the sky was lit up with lights and lamps, and the stars were so faint. I looked for Na'sh and his daughters, I looked for Venus in the gloomy night skies. I looked for the consorts of the moon, but all I could see was pale yellow sky far away, and the light of the lamps reflected in the mirrors spoiled everything. When I told Anne this, she said: "You are untamable. This is civilization." Then she said with a greater air of practicality: "You'll get used to everything. Then you won't feel so lonely." All the servants had white skin and blond hair, and they jabbered away with her in their own language. I just felt more alone; no one to keep me company, no one to sit with.

Then she said: "Do you want to learn?" and everything began to have an appointed time.

The doctor with the sickly face undid my bandages and changed the dressing. Every time after he finished he would go and solemnly confer with her. Her face was without expression and I couldn't understand. I told her I was in pain, as if a swarm of greedy ants were eating my leg. She didn't reply.

Khayra became pregnant. "A rare line," Anne said. The little gazelle was in the next stall. They carried me to see her. Sometimes I would kiss Khayra tenderly between the eyes. She was going to be a mother. The gazelle's eyes, which looked like Zahwa's, were always tearful. "Good moorneeng— comment ça va—tri biyen."

I began to pick up more words. My eyes were opened to the mystery of letters "Ah ee . . . je m'appelle Fatim."

The doctor with the round glasses over his age-weary eyes always grumbled with displeasure and did not hide his irritation. When my father came, wearing his *igaal*, his eyes were swollen and red. He kissed me and lifted me onto his leg. Was he crying? She closed the door and I heard snippets of their whispered conversation. "I'm afraid there's no alternative. Otherwise take her home with you now, and in a couple of months I'll come to offer my condolences." I understood.

He went out broken and confused. They were talking in loud voices about racing and shipping and import. She wanted to take him to the stables. As she was going out she said, "Your filly is stubborn, but she's sweet." He smiled and his smile alighted on my face with grief and sadness. He left. The next time I saw him I was wrapped in white bandages. I felt for my leg, but I couldn't find it. I looked at him and saw the tears, tears which he was not hiding. Now I really was "the cripple" and there was nothing I could do to avoid the name.

I called Zahwa, but she didn't answer. I knocked on the marble-covered floor with my crutch, but nothing came out except fear and loneliness. Get out of here, ya-Zahwa. It's me, Fatim the cripple. I talked to the eyes hanging on my chest and I continued my education. "Ah, gee, oh." Now I was able to understand some words and sometimes I tried to communicate. I would sit on the large verandah, which looked out over the Nile, and watch the palm trees swaying in the distance, and I would weep. "O palm tree standing tall in my father's house, are your bunches of dates ripe?" I would sing and she would clap her hands as if we were putting on a performance.

I cried at night. I dreamed I saw a horned viper chasing Zahwa. She was screaming. The viper was small, sand-colored, and blind. The shepherds cowered in fear when they heard its hiss, and the desert prayed silently to God. She saw the viper fly through the air. Someone would be bitten and a limb would surely be lost, a hand, a foot, a leg. Zahwa ran and ran as the hissing grew louder. "Run, ya-Zahwa, run so they won't cut your leg off like they did with Fatim the cripple. Hide somewhere. The desert's flat and open, nowhere to hide. Hide in the well, ya-Zahwa . . . Run!"

I woke up. It was the damp patch between my legs that woke me. The servant had put a rug under me to soak it up, and every morning she would take the pungent-smelling thing outside and dry it in the sun.

I didn't like playing the instrument that looked like a crocodile from the lakes on the Nile. I didn't like the ringing sound it made. "Don't make me learn it."

"As you like," Anne said.

But when her many guests came round in the evenings, and their glasses were filled and the conversation flowed, Anne would dress me up in one of the cloaks that Mouha had embroidered with bright colors. My plaits almost reached down to my ankles, and sometimes one of them would get trapped under my crutch and I would yell.

Anne said: "Your hair has grown so long."

I told her that the ugly genie had tattooed the key of life on my eyelid, and had said that my hair would grow longer than the hair of Sitt al-Hosn, whose plaits hung down from the window of the tower. Anne smiled greedily. She loved my stories, and nothing delighted her more than listening to them. It was as if she were discovering new and wonderful things with me.

Safiya's face looked down on me in my dreams. It was beautiful and round, glowing with health, and free of cares.

Rihana and Fouz were whispering to one another, Sardoub combed my hair while Sasa poured the water. Zahwa never left my side.

I told Anne that Zahwa never left my side. She lived underneath me wherever I went, and her netherworldly soul dwelled in the eyes of the little gazelle. Anne chuckled with pleasure as I hobbled before her guests with my plaits and my cloak. The guests would gather round me. "Hey, ya-Fatim, say something. Sing a song, ya-Fatim."

They would gaze at me with curious eyes full of amazement and I would sing.

> *I would look into the distance, far away from*
> *their din and sing:*
> *Lord Despair, Lady Distance,*
> *You have us surrounded.*
> *Lord Despair and Lady Distance*
> *And seven wounds; they all frighten me,*
> *And while he was away,*
> *His love grew in my heart,*
> *But the Master never brought him back,*
> *And he left me nothing but*
> *These wounds.*

They gasped, they didn't understand anything. Anne said: "Tell them."

I said: "Despair and separation are always with us, and how often it is written that we should part. God has decreed that it should be so for those who love, and my loved ones have left nothing but wounds in my heart."

They applauded. Anne said: "You were wonderful, ya-Fatim. You speak fluently." She said it admiringly and she went on: "She couldn't even read or write in her own language, and now she knows three languages. She reads a lot. We have worked out a special program for her education."

They smiled in astonishment and heaped praise upon her. She told them about her research, in which she was recording her observations of Bedouin life. She listed her interests: horses, hawks, hunting, woman. She went on about it at length, and they questioned her with great interest. I withdrew inside myself, searching for Musallam's bucket so he could let it down the well and I could hang on. I felt that my existence was like that of the birds in their cages and Khayra in her stall.

"Tell us a story, ya-Fatim."

What can Fatim the cripple tell you? I sighed, and the tattoo on my chin shone as they opened their mouths.

"Tattoos on the skin tell the same story. Every girl sees in her sleep a horseman or a lion, but this time it was a camel Sigeema saw while she was asleep. His eyes were two waterwheels, his body a barren hillside, his hump a tent, his legs tent pegs planted deep into the bowels of the pastureland. She saw him grazing on the tips of her plaits. She thought that perhaps it was a sign of death, but his eyes turned forlornly to the sand dunes. He said to her: 'The camels, after they had been patient, and had eaten from the wild desert grasses, and their humps had grown thin, despised the hobble and the halter and the bridle.' Then he sank to his knees. She arose from her submissive slumber, and when she reached out her hand and untied the nose band which was restraining him, he bent his long neck and pulled off the ropes that bound his legs. Then he sped off into the desert and never returned."

I would interrupt the stories and explain them, and I would pause and repeat. "The slave is a slave and the horseman is a wanderer, but he was neither slave nor horseman. He looked like the priest who visited the church on the Coptic Mountain. He raised his cross while the men sat around him on their horses and the shepherds waved palm fronds in the air. That priest in his white garments was comely and dignified, unlike the Copts, whose custom it was to dress themselves in black. Sigeema was most astonished that day when she saw the Arab horsemen taking his hand and kissing it and then wiping their own hands on their clothes to preserve the blessing. Every time she saw Musallam when she was young, she remembered that priest, who had never come back. Or perhaps he had come back and she had not seen him, for they were always on the move. Whenever a place grew tired of them, or they grew tired of it, they would move on in search of fresh pastures."

The guests smiled, captivated by my eloquence. Anne continued to encourage me: "The story, ya-Fatim, tell the story."

"Such dignity and refinement had moved her heart from the first moment. Her people, like their cousins, the Ma'aaza Arabs, had neither property nor weapons. They braced their shoulders to support the feet of the horseman as he mounted, and then they would look after his ewes. The slave is a slave, but the horseman may wander where he will. Sigeema had learned this fact the moment her eyes had been opened to the backbreaking work of gathering dung, grinding corn, churning milk, shearing the goats and sheep and washing the wool, and weaving it into carpets and compartments for the tent.

"And before that she had wandered far into the desert in search of grazing. Her hands had known the roughness of life, and in this she was not alone. But her short, thin body and her agility made her skillful in all things. No one knew how he had noticed her, but she understood that her feet, as they skipped along the pastureland behind the flock, left tracks that resembled those of a wild rabbit as it darted between the dunes and hollows. She also had a sweet, mellow voice and the women would gather round her at night to listen to her singing their praises. She would extol the qualities of each one and celebrate her beauty.

"She wandered far and wide with her songs, and laughed, and her teeth were worn down like the teeth of mountain rabbits who are always nibbling rough thorns. When he came she stepped out of the tent, lowering her veil to reveal half an almond-shaped eye, which shone brightly. Then she walked past the place where he was sitting, while the women standing with the flocks laughed at her impossible desire that the dignified gentleman would fall into the trap of a poor Bedouin woman with dusty clothes, and no luck with anything, not even the fat on her body. No one's clothes were as clean as his except that priest who dressed in white and had a silver crucifix hanging round his neck.

"Sigeema moved like a filly they were teaching to run. As she leaned slightly, the hem of her dress revealed her anklet and the ankle bone and the black tendons looked funny. One of the old men shooed her away from the shelter they had put up: 'Girl, stop cavorting about like a serpent. Go and see to your business.'

"The women laughed again as Sigeema ran toward them, full of anger and resentment at her wretched fortune, which seemed it was tied to the foot of a dusty bird of ill-omen that had never even landed on the earth."

"Carry on, ya-Fatim." I swallowed my saliva, licked my lips as I thought, and went on with the story.

"One day he chose her. He set up a vast tent, where the women sat weaving the rugs and carpets. He bought from them ewes, a small camel who looked like he'd just come out of his mother's belly, and a mule with two saddlebags to carry his belongings. And despite the little property and few animals he had, he went down in no one's estimation, especially when they learned that inside his shirt dangled a silver watch and a leather wallet full of notes and silver coins; for even the most important of their men had never known money or had any dealings with it. They were herdsmen, and their wealth was in the hands of the desert, which could bloom and sprout forth grazing so that they could rear and fatten their flocks, or which could

withhold its bounty that all might perish. After they
had spent time with him, and had come to know
him better, their admiration for him grew. Despite
his thin body, he was strong and could knock over
the most recalcitrant palm tree and split its trunk to
remove the white pith inside. If ever he was deep in
the desert and his waterskin was empty, he knew he
would find salvation in the palm trees which
inhabited the wilderness like houris from paradise.
He knew everything. If they asked him about the
caravans coming from the Nile, he would tell them
in which months they passed and the names of the
merchants and the markets where they traded.
Sigeema was also in awe of him, and his kindness
toward her touched her heart. She no longer had to
do so much backbreaking work. It was true that she
had no one to help her, but she was now the wife of
a respectable man who could plant shoots and graft
palm trees so well that he became, in the view of all
those who came across him, a man more blessed
than the priest in his white robes.

"Sigeema's belly swelled with child and he
couldn't believe it. He had given up hope of ever
having a son. When she gave birth to a daughter, he
loved her even more than Na'sh had loved his
daughters. He was extremely protective of her and
he kept her out of sight, hiding her like the
Pharaohs hid their treasure. The girl compensated
Sigeema for being separated from her own family,
who had moved elsewhere, and she was a noise in
the absolute silence of the empty patch of desert
where they were camped. Every new moon or two

a caravan would pass by. At such times Sigeema would be busy, kneading dough and lighting fires under her cooking pots to prepare food for the guests.

"There was nothing she enjoyed more than the pilgrimage caravans, when she could meet Egyptian women from across the Nile. They were plump with light-brown faces, and sat astride the camel litters, clothed in white. They would come and sit in the tent with her and they would chat at great length. When she laughed, her lips revealed her worn-down teeth. She would ask them to say prayers for her in the Holy Places, and sometimes, on their way back, they would bring her clothes from the Hijaz, or silver bracelets. Rarely did they forget to bring Javanese incense or a small bottle of musk from Mecca. Her happiness with these gifts was beyond description. She kept them in her chest and treated them with reverence. From time to time she would take them out and touch them, and say: 'Perfume for my funeral.'

"Every day that Zahwa grew, old age crept up on Musallam. His wrinkles became more pronounced and fears crowded in on his heart. From the time Zahwa began to crawl, he was often lost in thought and stayed up at night. He would hover around her compartment of the tent and no longer wandered off east or west. He said to Sigeema: 'I dream about Zahwa with the blood pouring from her beating heart and twisting in a thin trickle down between her legs.' Sigeema sighed: 'My dear husband, the fates have no ruse to alter the decrees of Him who separates the day from the night.' He buried his head in his hands. White hairs had covered his arms. He said: 'The desert is the lair of a howling wolf.' The wind whistled with pain, and as Sigeema wrapped her baby girl in rags and charms and prayers, she sang, oblivious to everything:

Moon, moon, a face giving light like the moon,
She's as bright as a star,
Shines in the night, then moves on.

I opened my eyes, and then closed them again, and swallowed my saliva as they looked on in amazement.

"Then came that swirling sandstorm. Sigeema said it was the genies of the desert. She did not fear the violent winter floods, and always said: 'Floods have their courses, but the swirling dust of the desert always snatches a loved one away.' This time Sigeema took refuge in her compartment of the tent, with incantations to bless the walls. They did not come out till the storm had died down. The dust dispersed in a burst of blazing summer heat above the writhing sand. But that dust must have taken someone away. And indeed it had. It went on swirling round and round and then began its retreat. It took Musallam, who had disappeared without a single trace."

Anne commented: "Nice story. What a clever girl you are!"

She took a while to explain to her guests. And when I hobbled up to my room, I felt my seven wounds. Zahwa, where are you? No answer. But then I saw her on the top of a hill that looked like a camel's hump. She was wounded and slept. Blood flowed from the wound down between her breasts and coagulated between her legs. I wept, and the blind, sand-colored viper hissed. They were amputating my leg. The wetness between my legs had a pungent smell. I put my rug in the sun and dried my tears.

Chapter Ten

Eyes, why are you shedding tears of mourning?

I told Anne that Sigeema was dead, that the slave was plucking out the feathers of the old she-falcon crucified on the tent peg. I told her that Musallam had gone away, I told her that Zahwa was wailing, she'd undone her braids, and there was a bird singing, but her heart was bleeding.

She made a brusque movement of her hand and carried on filling her pages while she asked me questions. I refused to answer. I'd had enough. You write. I watched her write. She wrote about Mouha and Sasa and Sardoub. She wrote about my mother and Safiya. She wrote about Dawwaba and her spells. I was sick of it. I am not a frog in a crystal jar for you to gaze upon. I am Fatim, ya-Anne, flesh and blood. Look at the cloaks that are now too small for me. Look at the open eyes on my chest. It's Zahwa's necklace. Seven wounds that weep in the night and wake me up. Don't applaud Fatim the cripple. I'm not going to sing. I'm not going to perform Bedouin folk songs. And I don't want to jabber away in any language. All I will do is wail like the ravens of doom. And the only tears that will flow from my eyes will be those of your gazelle, which has stopped eating.

My father didn't come. From the day they amputated my leg, he didn't appear. He didn't want to see me. I hobbled about on my crutch and there was no one to pick me up and carry me. Why wouldn't he come? Anne, won't you ever stop filling all those pages? Why won't you stop? Khayra grew weary from all the young she bore. A German stallion and an Arab mare, a filly with English fetlocks and an Arab back. Every year she would produce a new breed.

Are you fed up, Khayra, like me? Books and writing paper, pregnancy and labor.

The little gazelle died after it stopped eating. Anne said: "Gazelles don't have souls."

She had fat, white cats which I didn't like; I felt they were sluggish and grumpy.

I became paler and more bewildered. The garden wall closed in on me and I found the place stifling, unbearable. I could stand it no more and I wept bitterly. I sent letters to my father. "Have you forgotten Fatim?"

When he arrived he embraced me. "Come here, my princess. You've turned into a beautiful young woman."

I laughed. "A beautiful young woman cripple who hobbles about on a crutch with an amputated leg."

He kissed me affectionately between the eyes.

"I want to go away with you," I said.

He squeezed me tightly. "Your home always awaits your arrival, my darling gazelle."

Anne kissed me affectionately too. "Don't stay away too long." I nodded my head.

The house was the same as ever. There were a few more rugs in the rooms, and Dawwaba's daughter, Samawaat, had grown. She greeted me and kissed my hand. Everyone called her Nouma. I looked at her and smiled. Sardoub could not get up off her rug. Her legs were too swollen. She had them stretched out in front of her in humble resignation, but her heart was still beating and she called to me: "Fatim, Fatim, come here."

I kissed her.

"Ah, your hair has really grown, ya-Fatim, it's so long." They fingered my twisted plaits that dragged along the floor behind me. I looked at them closely. Dawwaba had left. He had avoided her until eventually she went back to her father's house. Every time he went on one of his journeys, she had borne him a stillborn son. She said: "This house is haunted. No boys will ever live in it."

They built her a house out by the fields, and they still died. She lost four sons. In the end she said to him: "Your offspring are cursed. You will never father a son, even if you marry all the daughters of the Arabs."

So he divorced her and got out of the house. Then came that thin, black woman called Rahaat. She was extremely thin and tall, but very kind. She spoke in a soft, low voice, and when she kissed me, she said, "Daughter and cousin." I smiled at her. In the main room they had put cupboards made of dark wood and fitted with mirrors, as well as new chairs. Despite all these outward changes, though, the place remained the same. I went into my room. The bed, the window, the wooden floor were all the same, as were the pigeon tower and the dome-shaped grainstores in the corner. And there was Grandmother Hakima's mother-of-pearl chest. I sat down in front of it and opened it. Inside were her cloaks and her blue dresses embroidered with mother-of-pearl.

Rahaat said with a sad sigh: "May God have mercy on the souls of our dead and the dead of all the Muslims. Your grandmother was a good woman who always prayed, and she died in the Holy Places."

I smiled, and she continued: "They buried her over there in the Land of Goodness. God have mercy on all of us."

I hobbled around the house and had a good look at it. I had a good look at Fouz and Rihana too, just as they were keen to have a good look at me. They opened my city clothes and laughed, but then they embraced me warmly. Safiya saw how I was walking and wept. Safiya was older, but her face was still fresh and plump. They reeled off the names of their children for me, but I forgot them straight away and I felt, despite all the signs of joy, a great loneliness and a deep sadness. I rested my head on the ground and yelled: "Zahwa!" She didn't come. I could still see her butchered body on some hilltop

or other, and Na'sh's daughters fled into the sky as
Sigeema groaned inside the tent.

Sigeema would uncover her hair in the blazing
heat of the desert sun, and sit there with her head
uncovered. The wrinkles of her sadness furrowed
deep in her face. She said that Musallam appeared to
her sometimes. The sands would part and he would
step out, with his headscarf let down over his
shoulders and his proud face smiling with kindness.
Then she would fall into silence and painful wailing,
and no one was able to stop her madness when
Zahwa tied her up inside the tent with the help of
the slave who had now grown up. She just
screamed and wailed, and it became clear to them
that she would die, whether she were tied up or left
free to roam where she wanted. She was like one
running toward her death, and the desert sun shows
no mercy to its victims. The woman's head became
a mass of blazing flame, pouring with sweat, her
reddened eyes dripping tears of bright red blood
and her swollen eyelids oozing with pain.

Tomorrow she will be incapable of doing
anything. She won't be able to uncover her head, or
run, or sit in the blazing sun, waiting. Zahwa
pounded herbs for her and moistened her parched
lips with the infusion, but it was all in vain. Sigeema
was nearing her end. She groaned in agony as Zahwa
changed the moistened rags that cooled her legs,
and bright red blood flowed from her backside and
down her legs, and scorching sweat poured down
her face.

Sigeema said she had seen Musallam. The sand dune split in two and out it came, the young camel that he had bought when they were married, before the sandstorm snatched it away. She went out to meet it every morning, collecting wild herbs in her lap. She took off its halter and undid her wrap as it moved its lips toward her, but it would not eat. It licked the ends of her plaits with its tongue, and then it departed as it had come, from the belly of the desert where secret things lie hidden. She crawled slowly to the dune. The impetuous sun climbed into the sky, ready to finish off its prey, as she rolled down the dune and half unconscious was barely able to scramble back to the flap of the tent before she crumpled to the ground. I looked at her exhausted face and I could find no new tears in my eyes. I remembered her running here and there, collecting horse manure and spinning sheep's wool, hurrying breathlessly between lighting fires and checking on the goats.

She was always there doing something or other, laughing with her worn-down rabbit teeth, running like a wild goat. All she ever did was run, as if her legs did not know how to walk. She was sprightly and compassionate, and in her eyes was a goodness and nobility. When we picked her up her body was as light as a feather. The wind shrieked and twisted round on itself and made a hole in the sand. But no well was there, no shoots would be planted. It was a hole, the size of her short, thin body, where she could lay down her head and sleep. And there was a young camel nibbling the remains of her plaits, which had turned to dust in the hot sun.

Chapter Eleven

Caught between despair and hope,
Why, my dear, did you leave me so?

The days were all very much alike. I had been away so long that a barrier seemed to have fallen between us. I decided to stay in the lemon room. My mother's bed was still there. I moved Grandmother Hakima's chest into the room. I smiled. Time is the healer of all pains. I looked at the trunk and there were no bad memories, perhaps even some affection. It didn't matter anymore. My heart was a lake of dried salt, shimmering in the distance, without waves or life. The walls of the room were full of cracks where the mud had split. Tiny mice fed in the wood of the ceiling and floor. I could hear them nibbling all day and night.

Sardoub dragged over her rug. The sound of her breathing slowly soothed me. Sasa came with a flock of quarreling children in tow. I asked her about Mouha, and she laughed and said: "The Gypsies have no land, only tents that they put up and take down. Then they pack them on their backs and move on."

She spoke with the common sense of a woman full of experience and life. She left me as I ran my fingers through my long hair and looked for Sardoub's folded lap. I leaned over and tears welled in my eyes.

My father came. He'd stopped going off on his journeys, and had put up his tent in the courtyard, by the guest house, and that was where he lived. He said that the closed-up rooms in our house were haunted with insomnia, and that he could only sleep soundly outside, in the open air. They would unroll his rugs for him and he would take off his headcloth and lie down and sleep. When the dew fell, he would stir and come and sit next to me.

"Why don't you live in your father's house, my princess?"

I laughed. "Why don't *you* live in it?"

"I can't stand the closed rooms." He hugged me and then started to talk to me, freely, like a child. He told me of his journeys, of the lions he had encountered. For a while he was lost in his own thoughts; and then he spoke again. "Fatim, my dear princess, look at Na'sh's daughters, look at the heavens."

I didn't answer. Fatim, the deaf-mute cripple. He left me to the croaking of the frogs and the chirping of the cockroaches, to the silence, and the hum of the mosquitoes.

I looked down into my lap, burying my head in paper. I felt that the letters were creatures of the night, roaming over my body, weighing it down. What is Fatim doing with letters, with words, when the loneliness is excruciating? Fouz and Rihana were busy with their children and I wondered if they still embroidered their dresses with beads and bright colors. Safiya arrived, with a slave and a donkey with two saddlebags walking behind her. She poked her stick all round the house, she went into the storerooms and the kitchen and the kneading room, with Aunt Rahaat trailing submissively behind her. She asked about the pigeons that had sprouted first fluff, and the eggs that had hatched, and the grain that had still to be ground. She prodded her stick into every cranny in the house and gave orders. I laughed as Fouz looked at her nervously, and said: "Like father like son."

She chuckled. "Girl, I'm your paternal aunt now, as well as your sister. The caravan can't move without a camel driver."

I let her drive all the camels she wanted, and wave her stick about. Our eyes met when I was hobbling along on my crutch, with the stump of my leg stuck out from under my dress. I saw the sorrow in her eyes. She saw where I was sleeping and waved her hands in dismay. "How can you sleep in this hole?"

I didn't reply, and she screamed: "The house is empty. It belongs to you and your father."

I mumbled, slowly but deliberately: "I can't stand the house."

Safiya shook her head and looked accusingly at Rahaat. "How can Fatim, the daughter of noble men, sleep in a nest of mice?"

I interrupted her ranting. "The house is cramped and stifling, and the rooms are haunted with insomnia."

Safiya said nothing, but the next morning some workmen came round. They tore out the wood and filled the cracks in the walls, plastered them with mud, then whitewashed them. I did not protest. It made no difference to me. I was a crow hopping about in the wilderness, and life was lonely and miserable.

The peasant girls sang as they passed the mud to the workmen.

Dawn's here and I haven't slept a wink.
Dawn's here . . .

Sardoub pressed her hand on my back and I glimpsed a vision of isolation.

My father came and sat down next to me on the balcony, on the carpet that had been spread out. He smiled as the sky scattered its stars. "Your house is looking beautiful, ya-Fatim. Tomorrow I'll plant you a couple of trees. Have you been writing to Anne, ya-Fatim? She's been asking about you."

I didn't say anything. What could I write to her? That Fatim had split in two, one half jabbering away in foreign languages and the other singing traditional Bedouin folk songs?

He cut my silence. "Why don't you say anything, ya-Fatim? Don't you like my company?"

I didn't like anything anymore.

He asked me again. "What's the matter with you, my princess?" Heartbreak showed in his eyes.

'I'm sad, Father, and alone, and miserable. I'm going round and round in a void. Zahwa has fallen in love with the bird of death, Musallam has gone away, and Sigeema has withered and died. Life has turned into a dusty wind and I am crucified like the she-falcon on the tent peg.' Should I tell him that? Would he really understand me if I told him? I started to delight in the game of silence, and I wondered what would happen if I stopped speaking altogether.

The night, dreary as usual, no one exists except you, ya-Fatim, desolate and alone. The day's commotion has died down. The main gate is ajar. They have not closed it or opened it for ages. Its bolts have fallen off and its bottom scrapes against the dusty ground. Now it remains ajar day and night. I decided to get out. Where could I go? I just hobbled along and looked around. His tent was still pitched in the space by the guest house. His body was wrapped in a blanket. One hand supported his cheek, while the other poked the embers of the slumbering fire.

I sat down next to him. I threw my crutch to one side and supported myself on his hand, which came up to meet me. "Fatim, sweetheart, what's bothering you? Why aren't you asleep?"

My eyes peered out into the emptiness. I felt afraid. His head, resting on my amputated leg, was covered in white hair. I looked at him more closely. The regular breathing scared me.

I set off down the path that wound between the wall of the house and the wall of the guest's quarters. Tree branches hung over the wall of our house and cast shadows. I hobbled along for a while, and the darkness grew thicker. I came to the canal, lined on either side by rustling reeds. Silence. Howling genies ran twisting through the swirls of mist, laughing, throwing stones at Fatim the cripple. "Zahwa, where do you live now? Ya-Zahwa, if only I knew how to explain to you."

I listened. Sardoub was looking for me. I heard her voice calling. "Ya-Fatim, where have you wandered off to this time, my daughter?"

I could hear her as I hobbled down the steps, down to the bottom of the well. I sat down. The sky above was like a narrow window. I could hear tiny creatures rummaging in their crevices, and the hiss of the blind viper rent my ears. "Fatim, the well's haunted, my child. Come to Sardoub."

I'm coming now. There's no one here anymore. The sound of the millstones with their pharaonic engravings rang in my ears, and as the two great stones rubbed together, blood oozed out from between them. My mother's blood, Zahwa's blood, Sigeema's blood drying in the sun.

Stop tormenting me, ya-Sardoub. If you don't stop, I'll strangle you with my bare hands. I'll strangle you with your black wrap. I'll strangle you with the torn-out tail of the filly.

I reached the bottom and Zahwa came. I sat down. The dew ate my flesh and I grew thinner and thinner. I felt my face.

Have you turned into an old woman, ya-Fatim? "Tri biyen." It's all over. When the worms eat your tongue, will they know how fluently you spoke? If only I knew where the worms come from. I dug in the dirt, scraping with both my hands, but I couldn't see any worms until I looked at the bottom of the rotten, decaying well and saw them crawling over my corpse.

No. Don't come and sit next to me. I won't speak to anybody, do you hear? I won't speak to anybody. Go to Samawaat's house and let her speak to you. Let her wipe the saliva from the corner of your mouth and shoo away the children from your sight.

"What is making you so sad, ya-Fatim, my child?"

No. You wouldn't understand anything. I hate you. If only I knew how to hate you, I would, and I would let all the bitter, corrupted blood pour out of my heart and go and live in Anne's house forever. I move on and evil thoughts pursue me. I threw away my crutch and went back to crawling. Sardoub's voice followed me everywhere. "Stand up, ya-Fatim. Get up out of the dirt, ya-Fattoum. Stand up, Sardoub's little darling."

No. I won't stand up, not even if Dawwaba's daughters come and stand round me and clap their hands in celebration, and make fun of me. Even if that Samawaat, whom he loves so much, comes and supports me, I won't stand up. I'll just crawl through burning desert that scorches my leg as I drag it along. Zahwa, where are you? I lifted up the rug and dug a hole in the sand. I buried the blood-soaked rags and looked around. Nothing but emptiness, and silence, and the sad mutterings of the wind as it whirled about on itself and made holes in the sand.

I said to Zahwa: "Come on, let's run away, into the burning, open desert, where the shifting sands will obliterate every trace."

Astonished, her wide, kohl-lined eyes opened to some distant spot on the horizon. She was waiting for Musallam. Perhaps his camel would be kneeling there at the door of the tent. He would open his cloak and embrace her, and light would shine through his fingers from his rosary, whose beads she sucked in her mouth like a tender nipple. Sigeema might be there too, crawling, skipping like a wild rabbit, waiting to rub Zahwa's legs with all the perfumed oils she had saved up in her chest, and sing to her.

> *Take her, she's from a line of princes,*
> *A free woman, doesn't like to do harm.*
> *Her beauty would disturb a saint,*
> *She moves like a gazelle,*
> *Graceful as an antelope,*
> *And she's clever with words too.*

Sigeema would do Zahwa's plaits for her and cross her legs so that Zahwa could rest her head on them, and kiss her on her forehead to make her sleep. She was waiting for that pure-white bird to return. The one Musallam saw in all his dreams from the day Zahwa learned to crawl, circling in the sky above the old she-falcon that had her wings trussed up her back. Every autumn the white bird would dig two holes, and springs of blood would gush forth and not dry up. Musallam spread out his nets, and laid his snares, and sharpened stones for his slingshot, and waited for the ground to swallow up the bird, or for the sky to toss it far away.

Zahwa was still waiting too. But now she no longer sat affectionately at his feet. The beads on his rosary no longer lit up her life. After he had worked hard setting the traps and the bird had not fallen into them, she said to him: "The sky isn't far away for one who has wings."

He held her in his arms and felt her small breasts trembling with passion. He kissed her forehead, and then the moon was on its way. She never saw him again, though Abou Shreek said later that Zaza, the Turkish wife, deserved to be killed, and that Musallam had gone back to cut up her body and throw it to the stray dogs, for she still boasted that she was better than him. She had even made fun of his manhood, and he had left her in the first place to get away from her wicked and malicious tongue.

Sigeema was thin and covered in tattoos, but she was noble and proud, and chaste of spirit. She loved him deeply and would follow him through the desert, wherever his feet would take him. She could not live without him. After he died, she gave herself up to the blazing sun until her veins burst and her blood dried up. Abou Shreek said all sorts of things to the pilgrimage caravans that passed and stopped at the well, where they would find nothing but a ragged tent with a woman wailing inside.

Chapter Twelve

When will the wind change,
And bring some welcome rain,
After all this dusty heat
And swirling sand?

"Why don't you open your windows?" Her beautiful eyes looked at me innocently, and I smiled. For a long time all they had seen on my face were emotionless scowls.

She was encouraged and came closer. "And why don't you go out?"

I would have laughed if I had known how. I stared more carefully at her face. Do you really look like my mother, ya-Samawaat, ya-Nouma, you little girl? Then why don't I look like her? No, in fact I had become exactly like her. I had entered the chamber of sobbing silence. The same swollen eyes. Maybe that's why the little girls were afraid of me when they gathered timidly around Sardoub's feet and she told them stories about camels and genies and kings. Maybe that was why my father had stopped coming.

She moved nearer to my hair: "Your hair's beautiful, ya-Fatim. Why don't you undo your plaits?"

I don't know why I didn't undo them. Perhaps I was no longer able to. It had grown much too long, longer than I could bear. It was like a tree trunk bending my neck backwards, holding it in a grip from which I could not escape.

I hobbled along by her side. The main gate was ajar. The dust had piled up and now it couldn't move. It was no longer opened and closed. A servant brought up the donkeys and sat the girls on them.

"Take good care of your daughters now, ya-Samawaat, my daughter."

The two little girls had grown. With their exercise books in their hands, they sat astride the donkeys, and the guard led them off to the school, which was far away on the other side of the hills. Rahaat watched them go with her thoughtful eyes, and then said: "Imagine, ya-Fatim, if your grandmother Hakima had seen this. She would have had their blood splashed on the doorway. The winds of time blow away all things in their wake."

I sighed. She heard the sound of my sigh. I hobbled toward the gate. As I approached its half-open edge I saw him. The wooden guest house was blackened by years of smoke and dirt, and time had settled its dust on the tent and carpets too. He sat there, and the men walked past and greeted him. He sighed and rubbed his fingers. He called her.

"Samawaat, Father's princess." When I heard that, I cried desperately, and the tears soaked my body. Had Fatim ceased to exist? Even your eyes no longer see me. Why have you abandoned your beloved? I went to the bottom of the well and sat down on the step and wailed until night fell, and Sardoub's voice came to me through the darkness: "Ya-Fatim, Fatima my dear, the well is haunted, my child ... Fatim, the night is treacherous. Ya-Fattoum, come to Sardoub, my precious darling."

I didn't answer. Fatim is her own darling and no one else's, darling of her own anger, and her own sad nights. I knew that her legs were incapable of carrying her and that her soft voice wouldn't stop calling until I went. I climbed up the steps of the well. The damned millstone wouldn't stop rumbling. It mixed with the endless hissing of the blind viper that was forever in pursuit. My eyes stayed open, even when I lay my head in her lap and she stroked my hair.

I heard my father calling for her. "Samawaat ... ya-Samawaat." Nouma ... ya-Nouma went and came between the half-open gate and his tent. His head was resting in her lap and he was telling her the story of Na'sh. Then he told her about Dawwaba, who had brought sand readers into his house to exorcise the evil of the curse which hung over the place. No boys, no sons. He told her of the red-faced Gurumi he had met, who looked neither like the Turks nor like the peasants. He had met the man on one of his travels and had told him that he was followed by a curse wherever he went. On moonlit nights the man would come and sit next to my father and talk to him about fate, and how the heavens write with the wind on the sand dunes the ends of all our journeys. The man sprinkled some pure sand in front of my father, and, with his eyes closed, blew. Then he read. "A hill, a dune, flatland, good, evil, darkness, mountains leading to a happy end."

And here he was now, leaning on her shoulder. She supported him as he walked, and he patted her back and proclaimed: "At least I have someone from my own flesh and blood to support me."

Then he became really old, just as Rahaat said. He would come and go between his tent and our house. I had thrown my crutch away, and whenever our eyes met as I crawled about, he turned his face away. He supported himself against her back so that he wouldn't stumble. She wiped the saliva from his mouth with the edge of her dress and cleaned the remains of sleep from the corners of his eyes and fed him pieces of bread soaked in milk with her own hands. He grew thinner and I crawled. I spent the day on the steps of the well and at night I would rest my head on Sardoub's leg. The rumble of the millstone and the hissing of the blind viper never left me. I crawled along between the tiny hills of sand that were scattered throughout the desert. A white bustard landed, then flew away again, just like the jasmine spreads out its petals and they fly and then fall to the ground, convulsing with exhaustion. I crawled on. No sign of life save a distant hum whose source I didn't know, and which had no effect on me. Neither genie nor human. An old abandoned well where Abou Shreek, wrapped in his white cloak, passed every year and leaned his head on a bare tent peg. Here in the past stood a tent in which a woman wailed.

"In the end," Abou Shreek said, "it was a camel. The king's wife gave birth to neither son nor daughter. It was a small camel. The camel grew up and married a woman who loved him, and he roamed through the pastures of her hair. Perhaps, when she was alone with him, he turned into a handsome prince, more handsome than anyone except the priest in his white robe. She bore him a daughter. The desert had never known one more beautiful."

After he had finished speaking, Abou Shreek threw the dregs of the coffee onto the dying embers and the pilgrims would set off behind him. They were no longer afraid when a wild rabbit skipped across the rocky path before them, or ran alongside with shining eyes, revealing behind its worn-down teeth the face of a woman, and a young camel grazing on her plaits.

And those who did not enjoy that story, if they made the pilgrimage the following year, would hear from Abou Shreek the story of Zaza, Musallam's Turkish wife, and what she had done to him. He would also tell them about his daughter, Zahwa, and how he worried about her if she even so much as winked or frowned. Everywhere they camped he would dig a hole behind the sand dunes, a grave for her, but every time he went to do the deed, pure

water gushed forth from the hole and he took it as a
sign from heaven that she should live. But the
Virgin in the sky took up her newborn child and set
off into the mountains. The pure water turned into
clotted blood, which flowed between Zahwa's
thighs. Abou Shreek finished off the story, swearing
that girls brought nothing but evil and that the grave
alone could protect a young woman's honor.

As I crawled along, the little girls pulled at my
hair. I felt they where whispering together in the
house: "The deranged woman's festering in the
well. Call her, ya-Sardoub."

"Ya-Fatim, come to Sardoub, your darling." No.
I won't come. Abou Shreek is coming. This time he
might say that the bird of death carried Zahwa away,
and that the pilgrims met an old woman who looked
like a wild rabbit, and a young camel running, and a
bleeding ewe followed by her lamb, and that the
pilgrims were used to these things by now. Don't
stroke my back. Don't touch me, ya-Sardoub. I
hate you and I hate Samawaat and I hate Rahaat. I
hate everything. Why do you drag me by my hair in
the night? Why do you tie it to those small tent
pegs? Why do you hang me up by my plaits? I
cannot bear the sound of the accursed millstone, or
my father's voice when he says: "Why don't you
open the door of your room, ya-Fatim? . . . Why
don't you use your crutch?" A crutch does not
conceal lameness. The crutch breaks my back. Do
you understand, ya-Samawaat, eh? Come on, get
out of the room, or I'll kick you good and hard. Get
out and go and see to his crooked back. Prop him

up if you wish. Fatim the cripple doesn't need anyone. "Fatim, my dear, why are you so sad? What has happened to you?"

Shut up, Sardoub, and be quiet! I don't want to hear a word from you. I can hear the girls outside making fun of Fatim. Those spoiled brats of Dawwaba's are making fun of my deformity. They say I'm possessed. But you, Sardoub, know the truth. You know Zahwa who lives at Musallam's oasis. Don't stroke my back. Why won't you admit you know her?

"Sleep, Fatim . . . Sleep, beautiful princess." No. I won't sleep. I know that you want to weave a tent out of my hair. You want Fatim to remain in the dark. I won't give up my plaits to you, ever. You just want me to die. I will die, ya-Sardoub, but get your hands away from my hair. Black hissing is everywhere, blind, sand-colored. When the shepherds hear that hissing, they cower in fear, and the desert hears it and prays silently to God. Fatim sees the viper fly through the air and land. Come on, come on . . .

You aren't afraid, are you? Don't worry, I'm not going to kill you. Just jump up and pour your poison here, between my eyes.

Modern Arabic Writing

from The American University in Cairo Press

Ibrahim Abdel Meguid *The Other Place* • *No One Sleeps in Alexandria*
Yahya Taher Abdullah *The Mountain of Green Tea*
Salwa Bakr *The Wiles of Men*
Mohamed El-Bisatie *Houses Behind the Trees* • *A Last Glass of Tea*
Fathy Ghanem *The Man Who Lost His Shadow*
Tawfiq al-Hakim *The Prison of Life*
Taha Hussein *A Man of Letters* • *The Sufferers* • *The Days*
Sonallah Ibrahim *Cairo: From Edge to Edge*
Yusuf Idris *City of Love and Ashes*
Said al-Kafrawi *The Hill of Gypsies*
Naguib Mahfouz *Adrift on the Nile*
Akhenaten, Dweller in Truth • *Arabian Nights and Days*
Autumn Quail • *The Beggar*
The Beginning and the End • *The Cairo Trilogy:*
Palace Walk • *Palace of Desire* • *Sugar Street*
The Day the Leader Was Killed • *Echoes of an Autobiography*
The Harafish • *The Journey of Ibn Fattouma*
Midaq Alley • *Miramar* • *Respected Sir*
The Search • *The Thief and the Dogs*
The Time and the Place • *Wedding Song*
Ahlam Mosteghanemi *Memory in the Flesh*
Abd al-Hakim Qasim *Rites of Assent*
Lenin El-Ramly *In Plain Arabic*
Rafik Schami *Damascus Nights*
Miral al-Tahawy *The Tent*